Sanditon

JANE AUSTEN'S

Unfinished Masterpiece Completed

JANE AUSTEN *and* JULIETTE SHAPIRO

Ulysses Press

Published in the United States by
ULYSSES PRESS
P.O. Box 3440
Berkeley, CA 94703
www.ulyssespress.com

ISBN: 978-1-56975-621-8
Library of Congress Catalog Number 2009900129

Cover design: TG Design
Cover illustration: *The Souvenir,* Jean-Honoré Fragonard/
The Granger Collection, New York
Editorial: Jennifer Privateer, Lauren Harrison
Production: Judith Metzener, Abigail Reser

Printed in Canada by Webcom

10 9 8 7 6 5 4 3 2 1

Distributed by Publishers Group West

Love with your hearts fully anchored,

love intensely.

for
Michael, Zoe, Emma and Cameron

and
Yasmin, Tristan, Carmen and Alissa

"Be not the slave of your own past. Plunge into the sublime seas, dive deep and swim far, so you shall come back with self-respect, with new power, with an advanced experience that shall explain and overlook the old."

Ralph Waldo Emerson

Introduction

Jane Austen began work on the draft we now know as Sanditon in January, 1817. She abandoned the project in March of the same year. Jane died on July 18, 1817, and since then many have wondered what she had in mind for her Sanditon characters. This story, my personal resolution to the unsolved mysteries of Sanditon, is written with every intention of remaining faithful to Jane Austen and entertaining those who, in longing to know more about her wonderful characters, find it in their hearts to forgive the impertinence of the sequelist.

CHAPTER 1

A gentleman and a lady traveling from Tunbridge toward that part of the Sussex coast which lies between Hastings and Eastbourne, being induced by business to quit the high road and attempt a very rough lane, were overturned in toiling up its long ascent, half rock, half sand. The accident happened just beyond the only gentleman's house near the lane, a house which their driver, on being first required to take that direction, had conceived to be necessarily their object and had with most unwilling looks been constrained to pass by. He had grumbled and shaken his shoulders and pitied and cut his horses so sharply that he might have been open to the suspicion of overturning them on purpose, especially as the carriage was not his master's own, if the road had not indisputably become worse than before, as soon as the premises of the said house were left behind—expressing with a most portentous countenance that, beyond it, no wheels but cart wheels could safely proceed.

The severity of the fall was broken by their slow pace and the narrowness of the lane; and the gentleman having scrambled out and helped out his companion, they neither of them at first felt more than shaken and bruised. But the gentleman had, in the course of the extrication, sprained his foot; and soon becoming sensible of it, was obliged in a few moments to cut short both his remonstrances to the driver and his congratulations to his wife and himself and sit down on the bank, unable to stand.

"There is something wrong here," said he, putting his hand to his ankle. "But never mind, my dear," looking up at her with a smile, "it could not have happened, you know, in a better place. Good out of evil. The very thing perhaps to be wished for. We shall soon get relief. There, I fancy, lies my cure," pointing to the neat-looking end of a cottage, which was seen romantically situated among wood on a high eminence at some little distance, "Does not that promise to be the very place?"

His wife fervently hoped it was; but stood, terrified and anxious, neither able to do or suggest anything, and receiving her first real comfort from the sight of several persons now coming to their assistance. The accident had been discerned from a hayfield adjoining the house they had passed. And the persons who approached were a well-looking, hale, gentlemanlike man of middle age, the proprietor of the place, who happened to be among his haymakers at the time, and three or four of the ablest of them summoned to attend their master, to say nothing of all the rest of the field, men, women, and children, not very far off. Mr. Heywood, such was the name of the said proprietor, advanced with a very civil salutation, much concern for the accident, some surprise at anybody's attempting that road in a carriage, and ready offers of assistance. His courtesies were received with good breeding and gratitude, and while one or two of the men lent their help to the driver in getting the carriage upright again, the traveler said, "You are extremely obliging Sir, and I take you at your word. The injury to my leg is, I daresay, very trifling. But it is always best in these cases, you know, to have a surgeon's opinion without loss of time; and as the road does not seem in a favorable state for my getting up to his house myself, I will thank you to send off one of these good people for the surgeon."

"The surgeon!" exclaimed Mr. Heywood. "I am afraid you will find no surgeon at hand here, but I daresay we shall do very well without him."

"Nay, Sir, if he is not in the way, his partner will do just as well, or rather better. I would rather see his partner. Indeed, I would prefer the attendance of his partner. One of these good people can be with him in three minutes, I am sure. I need not ask whether I see the house," looking toward the cottage, "for excepting your own, we have passed none in this place which can be the abode of a gentleman."

Mr. Heywood looked very much astonished. "What Sir! Are you expecting to find a surgeon in that cottage? We have neither surgeon nor partner in the parish, I assure you."

"Excuse me, Sir," replied the other. "I am sorry to have the appearance of contradicting you, but from the extent of the parish or some other cause you may not be aware of the fact. Stay. Can I be mistaken in the place? Am I not in Willingden? Is not this Willingden?"

"Yes, Sir, this is certainly Willingden."

"Then, Sir, I can bring proof of your having a surgeon in the parish, whether you may know it or not. Here Sir," taking out his pocket book, "if you will do me the favor of casting your eye over these advertisements which I cut out myself from the *Morning Post* and the *Kentish Gazette* only yesterday morning in London, I think you will be convinced that I am not speaking at random. You will find in it an advertisement of the dissolution of a partnership in the medical line, in your own parish; extensive business, undeniable character, respectable references, wishing to form a separate establishment. You will find it at full length, Sir," offering the two little oblong extracts.

"Sir, if you were to show me all the newspapers that are printed in one week throughout the kingdom, you would not persuade me of there being a surgeon in Willingden," said Mr. Heywood with a good-humored smile. "Having lived here ever since I was born, man and boy fifty-seven years, I think I must have known of such a person. At least I may venture to say that he has not much business. To be sure, if gentlemen were to be often attempting this lane in post chaises, it might not be a bad speculation for a surgeon to get a house at the top of the hill. But as to that cottage, I can assure you, Sir, that it is, in fact, in spite of its spruce air at this distance, as indifferent a double tenement as any in the parish, and that my shepherd lives at one end and three old women at the other." He took the pieces of paper as he spoke and, having looked them over, added, "I believe I can explain it, Sir. Your mistake is in the place. There are two Willingdens in this country. And your advertisements must refer to the other, which is Great Willingden or Willingden Abbots and lies seven miles off on the other side of Battle. Quite down in the weald. And we, Sir," he added, speaking rather proudly, "are not in the weald."

"Not down in the weald, I am sure," replied the traveler pleasantly. "It took us half an hour to climb your hill. Well, I daresay it is as you say and I have made an abominably stupid blunder. All done in a moment. The advertisements did not catch my eye till the last half hour of our being in town, everything in the hurry and confusion, which always attend a short stay there. One is never able to complete anything in the way of business, you know, till the carriage is at the door. So satisfying myself with a brief inquiry, and finding we were actually to pass within a mile or two of a Willingden, I sought no farther. My dear," to his wife, "I am very sorry to have brought you into this scrape. But do not be alarmed about my leg. It gives me no pain while I am quiet. And as soon as these good people have succeeded in setting the carriage to rights and turning the horses round, the best thing we can do will be to measure back our steps into the turnpike road and proceed to Hailsham, and so home without attempting anything farther. Two hours take us home from Hailsham. And once at home, we have our remedy at hand, you know. A little of our own bracing sea air will soon set me on my feet again. Depend upon it, my dear, it is exactly a case for the sea. Saline air and immersion will be the very thing. My sensations tell me so already."

In a most friendly manner Mr. Heywood here interposed, entreating them not to think of proceeding till the ankle had been examined and some refreshment taken, and very cordially pressing them to make use of his house for both purposes. "We are always well stocked," said he, "with all the common remedies for sprains and bruises. And I will answer for the pleasure it will give my wife and daughters to be of service to you in every way in their power."

A twinge or two, in trying to move his foot, disposed the traveler to think rather more than he had done at first of the benefit of immediate assistance; and consulting his wife in the few words of, "Well my dear, I believe it will be better for us." He turned again to Mr. Heywood. "Before we accept your hospitality, Sir, and in order to do away with any unfavorable impression which the sort of wild-goose chase you find me in may have given rise to, allow me to tell you who we are. My name is Parker, Mr. Parker of Sanditon. This lady, my wife, Mrs. Parker. We are on our road home from London. My name perhaps, though I am by no means the first of my family holding landed property in the parish of Sanditon, may be unknown at this distance from the coast. But Sanditon itself, everybody has heard of Sanditon. The favorite, for a young and rising bathing-place, certainly the favorite spot of all that are to be found along the coast of Sussex; the most favored by nature, and promising to be the most chosen by man."

"Yes, I have heard of Sanditon," replied Mr. Heywood. "Every five years, one hears of some new place or other starting up by the sea and growing the fashion. How they can half of them be filled is the wonder! Where people can be found with money and time to go to them! Bad things for a country, sure to raise the price of provisions and make the poor good for nothing, as I daresay you find, Sir."

"Not at all, Sir, not at all," cried Mr. Parker eagerly. "Quite the contrary, I assure you. A common idea, but a mistaken one. It may apply to your large, overgrown places like Brighton or Worthing or Eastbourne, but not to a small village like Sanditon, precluded by its size from experiencing any of the evils of civilization; while the growth of the place, the buildings, the nursery grounds, the demand for everything, and the sure resort of the very best company, those regular, steady, private families of thorough gentility and character who are a blessing everywhere, excite the industry of the poor and diffuse comfort and improvement among them of every sort. No, Sir, I assure you, Sanditon is not a place ..."

"I do not mean to take exception to any place in particular," answered Mr. Heywood. "I only think our coast is too full of them altogether. But had we not better try to get you ..."

"Our coast too full!" repeated Mr. Parker. "On that point perhaps we may not totally disagree. At least there are enough. Our coast is abundant enough. It demands no more. Everybody's taste and everybody's finances may be suited. And those good people who are trying to add to the number are, in my opinion, excessively absurd and must soon find themselves the dupes of their own fallacious calculations. Such a place as Sanditon, Sir, I may say, was wanted, was called for. Nature had marked it out, had spoken in most intelligible characters. The finest, purest sea breeze on the coast, acknowledged to be so, excellent bathing, fine hard sand, deep water ten yards from the shore, no mud, no weeds, no slimy rocks. Never was there a place more palpably designed by nature for the resort of the invalid, the very spot that thousands seemed in need of! The most desirable distance from London! One complete, measured mile nearer than Eastbourne. Only conceive, Sir, the advantage of saving a whole mile in a long journey. But Brinshore, Sir, which I daresay you have in your eye, the attempts of two or three speculating people about Brinshore this last year to raise that paltry hamlet, lying as it does between a stagnant marsh, a bleak moor, and the constant effluvia of a ridge of putrefying seaweed, can end in nothing but their own disappointment. What in the name of common sense is to recommend Brinshore? A most insalubrious air, roads proverbially detestable, water brackish beyond example, impossible to get a good dish of tea within three miles of the place. And as for the soil! It is so cold and ungrateful that it can hardly be made to yield a cabbage. Depend upon it, Sir, that this is a most faithful description of Brinshore, not in the smallest degree exaggerated, and if you have heard it differently spoken of …"

"Sir, I never heard it spoken of in my life before," said Mr. Heywood. "I did not know there was such a place in the world."

"You did not! There my dear," turning with exultation to his wife, "you see how it is. So much for the celebrity of Brinshore! This gentleman did not know there was such a place in the world. Why, in truth, Sir, I fancy we may apply to Brinshore that line of the poet Cowper in his description of the religious cottager, as opposed to Voltaire, '*She*, never heard of half a mile from home.'"

"With all my heart, Sir, apply any verses you like to it. But I want to see something applied to your leg. And I am sure by your lady's countenance that she is quite of my opinion and thinks it a pity to lose any more time. And here come my girls to speak for themselves and their mother."

Two or three genteel-looking young women, followed by as many maidservants, were now seen issuing from the house. "I began to wonder the bustle should not have reached them. A thing of this kind soon makes a stir in a lonely place like ours. Now, Sir, let us see how you can be best conveyed into the house."

The young ladies approached and said everything that was proper to recommend their father's offers and, in an unaffected manner, calculated to make the strangers easy. As Mrs. Parker was exceedingly anxious for relief, and her husband by this time not much less disposed for it, a very few civil scruples were enough; especially as the carriage, being now set up, was discovered to have received such injury on the fallen side as to be unfit for present use. Mr. Parker was therefore carried into the house and his carriage wheeled off to a vacant barn.

CHAPTER 2

The acquaintance, thus oddly begun, was neither short nor unimportant. For a whole fortnight the travelers were fixed at Willingden, Mr. Parker's sprain proving too serious for him to move sooner. He had fallen into very good hands. The Heywoods were a thoroughly respectable family and every possible attention was paid, in the kindest and most unpretending manner, to both husband and wife. He was waited on and nursed, and she cheered and comforted with unremitting kindness; and as every office of hospitality and friendliness was received as it ought, as there was not more goodwill on one side than gratitude on the other, nor any deficiency of generally pleasant manners in either, they grew to like each other in the course of that fortnight exceedingly well.

Mr. Parker's character and history were soon unfolded. All that he understood of himself, he readily told, for he was very openhearted; and where he might be himself in the dark, his conversation was still giving information to such of the Heywoods as could observe. By such he was perceived to be an enthusiast on the subject of Sanditon, a complete enthusiast. Sanditon, the success of Sanditon as a small, fashionable bathing place, was the object for which he seemed to live. A very few years ago, it had been a quiet village of no pretensions; but some natural advantages in its position and some accidental circumstances having suggested to himself and the other principal landholder the probability of its becoming a profitable speculation, they had engaged in it, and planned and built, and praised and puffed, and raised it to something of young renown; and Mr. Parker could now think of very little besides. The facts which, in more direct communication, he laid before them were that he was about five and thirty, had been married, very happily married, seven years, and had four sweet children at home; that he was of a respectable family and easy, though not large, fortune; no profession, succeeding as eldest son to the property which two or three generations had been holding and accumulating before him; that he had two brothers and two sisters, all single and all independent, the eldest of the two former indeed, by collateral inheritance, quite as well provided for as himself.

His object in quitting the high road to hunt for an advertising surgeon was also plainly stated. It had not proceeded from any intention of spraining his ankle or doing himself any other injury for the good of such surgeon, nor (as Mr. Heywood had been apt to suppose) from any design of entering into partnership with him; it was merely in consequence of a wish to establish some medical man at Sanditon, which the nature of the advertisement induced him to expect to accomplish in Willingden. He was convinced that the advantage of a medical man at hand would very materially promote the rise and prosperity of the place, would in fact tend to bring a prodigious influx; nothing else was wanting. He had strong reason to believe that one family had been deterred last year from trying Sanditon on that account, and probably very many more, and his own sisters, who were sad invalids and whom he was very anxious to get to Sanditon this summer, could hardly be expected to hazard themselves in a place where they could not have immediate medical advice.

Upon the whole, Mr. Parker was evidently an amiable family man, fond of wife, children, brothers, and sisters, and generally kindhearted, liberal, gentlemanlike, easy to please, of a sanguine turn of mind, with more imagination than judgment. And Mrs. Parker was as evidently a gentle, amiable, sweet-tempered woman, the properest wife in the world for a man of strong understanding but not of a capacity to supply the cooler reflection which her own husband sometimes needed; and so entirely waiting to be guided on every occasion that whether he was risking his fortune or spraining his ankle, she remained equally useless. Sanditon was a second wife and four children to him, hardly less dear, and certainly more engrossing. He could talk of it forever. It had indeed the highest claims; not only those of birthplace, property, and home; it was his mine, his lottery, his speculation, and his hobbyhorse; his occupation, his hope, and his futurity.

He was extremely desirous of drawing his good friends at Willingden thither; and his endeavors in the cause were as grateful and disinterested as they were warm. He wanted to secure the promise of a visit, to get as many of the family as his own house would contain to follow him to Sanditon as soon as possible; and, healthy as they all undeniably were, foresaw that every one of them would be benefited by the sea. He held it indeed as certain that no person could be really well, no person (however upheld for the present by fortuitous aids of exercise and spirits in a semblance of health) could be really in a state of secure and permanent health without spending at least six weeks by the sea every year. The sea air and seabathing together were nearly infallible, one or the other of them being a match for every disorder of the stomach, the lungs or the blood. They were antispasmodic, antipulmonary, antiseptic, antibilious, and antirheumatic. Nobody could catch cold by the sea; nobody wanted appetite by the sea; nobody wanted spirits; nobody wanted strength. Sea air was healing, softening, relaxing, fortifying, and bracing—seemingly just as was wanted—sometimes one, sometimes the other. If the sea breeze failed, the seabath was the certain corrective; and where bathing disagreed, the sea air alone was evidently designed by nature for the cure.

His eloquence, however, could not prevail. Mr. and Mrs. Heywood never left home. Marrying early and having a very numerous family, their movements had long been limited to one small circle; and they were older in habits than in age. Excepting two journeys to London in the year to receive his dividends, Mr. Heywood went no farther than his feet or his well-tried old horse could carry him; and Mrs. Heywood's adventurings were only now and then to visit her neighbors in the old coach which had been new when they married and fresh-lined on their eldest son's coming of age ten years ago. They had a very pretty property; enough, had their family been of reasonable limits, to have allowed them a very gentlemanlike share of luxuries and change; enough for them to have indulged in a new carriage and better roads, an occasional month at Tunbridge Wells, and symptoms of the gout and a winter at Bath, but the maintenance, education, and fitting out of fourteen children demanded a very quiet, settled, careful course of life, and obliged them to be stationary and healthy at Willingden. What prudence had at first enjoined was now rendered pleasant by habit. They never left home and they had gratification in saying so. But very far from wishing their children to do the same, they were glad to promote their getting out into the world as much as possible. They stayed at home that their children might get out, and, while making that home extremely comfortable, welcomed every change from it that could give useful connections or respectable acquaintance to sons or daughters.

When Mr. and Mrs. Parker, therefore, ceased from soliciting a family visit and bounded their views to carrying back one daughter with them, no difficulties were started. It was general pleasure and consent. Their invitation was to Miss Charlotte Heywood, a very pleasing young woman of two and twenty, the eldest of the daughters at home and the one who, under her mother's directions, had been particularly useful and obliging to them; who had attended them most and knew them best. Charlotte was to go, with excellent health, to bathe and be better if she could, to receive every possible pleasure which Sanditon could be made to supply by the gratitude of those she went with, and to buy new parasols, new gloves, and new brooches for her sisters and herself at the library, which Mr. Parker was anxiously wishing to support. All that Mr. Heywood himself could be persuaded to promise was that he would send everyone to Sanditon who asked his advice, and that nothing should ever induce him (as far as the future could be answered for) to spend even five shilling at Brinshore.

CHAPTER 3

Every neighborhood should have a great lady. The great lady of Sanditon was Lady Denham, and in their journey from Willingden to the coast, Mr. Parker gave Charlotte a more detailed account of her than had been called for before. She had been necessarily often mentioned at Willingden, for being his colleague in speculation, Sanditon itself could not be talked of long without the introduction of Lady Denham. That she was a very rich old lady, who had buried two husbands, who knew the value of money, and was very much looked up to and had a poor cousin living with her, were facts already known; but some further particulars of her history and her character served to lighten the tediousness of a long hill, or a heavy bit of road, and to give the visiting young lady a suitable knowledge of the person with whom she might now expect to be daily associating.

Lady Denham had been a rich Miss Brereton, born to wealth but not to education. Her first husband had been a Mr. Hollis, a man of considerable property in the country, of which a large share of the parish of Sanditon, with manor and mansion house, made a part. He had been an elderly man when she married him, her own age about thirty. Her motives for such a match could be little understood at the distance of forty years, but she had so well nursed and pleased Mr. Hollis that at his death he left her everything, all his estates, and all at her disposal. After a widowhood of some years, she had been induced to marry again. The late Sir Harry Denham, of Denham Park in the neighborhood of Sanditon, had succeeded in removing her and her large income to his own domains, but he could not succeed in the views of permanently enriching his family which were attributed to him. She had been too wary to put anything out of her own power and when, on Sir Harry's decease, she returned again to her own house at Sanditon, she was said to have made this boast to a friend, "that though she had got nothing but her title from the family, still she had *given* nothing for it." For the title, it was to be supposed, she had married and Mr. Parker acknowledged there being just such a degree of value for it apparent now as to give her conduct that natural explanation. "There is at times," said he, "a little self-importance, but it is not offensive, and there are moments, there are points, when her love of money is carried greatly too far. But she is a good-natured woman, a very good-natured woman, a very obliging, friendly neighbor, a cheerful, independent, valuable character and her faults may be entirely imputed to her want of education. She has good natural sense, but quite uncultivated. She has a fine active mind as well as a fine healthy frame for a woman of seventy, and enters into the improvement of Sanditon with a spirit truly admirable. Though now and then, a littleness will appear. She cannot look forward quite as I would have her and takes alarm at a trifling present expense without considering what returns it will make her in a year or two. That is, we think differently. We now and then see things differently, Miss Heywood. Those who tell their own story, you know, must be listened to with caution. When you see us in contact, you will judge for yourself."

Lady Denham was indeed a great lady beyond the common wants of society, for she had many thousands a year to bequeath, and three distinct sets of people to be courted by: her own relations, who might very reasonably wish for her original thirty thousand pounds among them; the legal heirs of Mr. Hollis, who must hope to be more indebted to her sense of justice than he had allowed them to be to his; and those members of the Denham family whom her second husband had hoped to make a good bargain for. By all of these, or by branches of them, she had no doubt been long, and still continued to be, well attacked; and of these three divisions, Mr. Parker did not hesitate to say that Mr. Hollis's kindred were the least in favor and Sir Harry Denham's the most. The former, he believed, had done themselves irremediable harm by expressions of very unwise and unjustifiable resentment at the time of Mr. Hollis's death; the latter had the advantage of being the remnant of a connection which she certainly valued, of having been known to her from their childhood and of being always at hand to preserve their interest by reasonable attention. Sir Edward, the present baronet, nephew to Sir Harry, resided constantly at Denham Park and Mr. Parker had little doubt that he and his sister, Miss Denham, who lived with him, would be principally remembered in her will. He sincerely hoped it. Miss Denham had a very small provision; and her brother was a poor man for his rank in society. "He is a warm friend to Sanditon," said Mr. Parker, "and his hand would be as liberal as his heart, had he the power. He would be a noble coadjutor! As it is, he does what he can and is running up a tasteful little cottage ornee on a strip of waste ground Lady Denham has granted him, which I have no doubt we shall have many a candidate for before the end even of this season." Till within the last twelvemonth, Mr. Parker had considered Sir Edward as standing without a rival, as having the fairest chance of succeeding to the greater part of all that she had to give. But there were now another person's claims to be taken into account, those of the young female relation whom Lady Denham had been induced to receive into her family.

After having always protested against any such addition, and long and often enjoyed the repeated defeats she had given to every attempt of her relations to introduce this young lady or that young lady as a companion at Sanditon House, she had brought back with her from London last Michaelmas a Miss Brereton, who bid fair by her merits to vie in favor with Sir Edward and to secure for herself and her family that share of the accumulated property which they had certainly the best right to inherit. Mr. Parker spoke warmly of Clara Brereton, and the interest of his story increased very much with the introduction of such a character. Charlotte listened with more than amusement now; it was solicitude and enjoyment, as she heard her described to be lovely, amiable, gentle, unassuming, conducting herself uniformly with great good sense, and evidently gaining by her innate worth on the affections of her patroness. Beauty, sweetness, poverty, and dependence do not want the imagination of a man to operate upon; with due exceptions, woman feels for woman very promptly and compassionately. He gave the particulars that had led to Clara's admission at Sanditon as no bad exemplification of that mixture of character, that union of littleness with kindness and good sense, even liberality, which he saw in Lady Denham.

After having avoided London for many years, principally on account of these very cousins who were continually writing, inviting, and tormenting her, and whom she was determined to keep at a distance, she had been obliged to go there last Michaelmas with the certainty of being detained at least a fortnight. She had gone to an hotel, living by her own account as prudently as possible to defy the reputed expensiveness of such a home, and at the end of three days calling for her bill that she might judge of her state. Its amount was such as determined her on staying not another hour in the house, and she was preparing, in all the anger and perturbation of her belief in very gross imposition and her ignorance of where to go for better usage, to leave the hotel at all hazards, when the cousins, the politic and lucky cousins, who seemed always to have a spy on her, introduced themselves at this important moment and, learning her situation, persuaded her to accept such a home for the rest of her stay as their humbler house in a very inferior part of London could offer. She went, was delighted with her welcome and the hospitality and attention she received from everybody, found her good cousins the Breretons, beyond her expectation, worthy people and finally was impelled by a personal knowledge of their narrow income and pecuniary difficulties to invite one of the girls of the family to pass the winter with her. The invitation was to one, for six months, with the probability of another being then to take her place. But in selecting the one, Lady Denham had shown the good part of her character for, passing by the actual daughters of the house, she had chosen Clara, a niece, more helpless and more pitiable of course than any, a dependent on poverty, an additional burden on an encumbered circle and one who had been so low in every worldly view as, with all her natural endowments and powers, to have been preparing for a situation little better than a nursery maid. Clara had returned with her and by her good sense and merit had now, to all appearance, secured a very strong hold in Lady Denham's regard.

The six months had long been over and not a syllable was breathed of any change or exchange. She was a general favorite. The influence of her steady conduct and mild, gentle temper was felt by everybody. The prejudices that had met her at first, in some quarters, were all dissipated. She was felt to be worthy of trust, to be the very companion who would guide and soften Lady Denham, who would enlarge her mind and open her hand. She was as thoroughly amiable as she was lovely and, since having had the advantage of their Sanditon breezes, that loveliness was complete.

CHAPTER 4

"And whose very snug looking place is this?" said Charlotte as, in a sheltered dip within two miles of the sea, they passed close by a moderate-sized house, well fenced and planted, and rich in the garden, orchard, and meadows which are the best embellishments of such a dwelling. "It seems to have as many comforts about it as Willingden."

"Ah," said Mr. Parker. "This is my old house, the house of my forefathers, the house where I and all my brothers and sisters were born and bred, and where my own three eldest children were born, where Mrs. Parker and I lived till within the last two years, till our new house was finished. I am glad you are pleased with it. It is an honest old place and Hillier keeps it in very good order. I have given it up, you know, to the man who occupies the chief of my land. He gets a better house by it, and I, a rather better situation! One other hill brings us to Sanditon. Modern Sanditon! A beautiful spot. Our ancestors, you know, always built in a hole. Here were we, pent down in this little contracted nook, without air or view, only one mile and three quarters from the noblest expanse of ocean between the South Foreland and Land's End, and without the smallest advantage from it. You will not think I have made a bad exchange when we reach Trafalgar House, which, by the by, I almost wish I had not named Trafalgar, for Waterloo is more the thing now. However, Waterloo is in reserve and if we have encouragement enough this year for a little crescent to be ventured on (as I trust we shall) then we shall be able to call it Waterloo Crescent and the name joined to the form of the building, which always takes, will give us the command of lodgers. In a good season we should have more applications than we could attend to."

"It was always a very comfortable house," said Mrs. Parker, looking at it through the back window with something like the fondness of regret. "And such a nice garden, such an excellent garden."

"Yes, my love, but that we may be said to carry with us. It supplies us, as before, with all the fruit and vegetables we want. And we have, in fact, all the comfort of an excellent kitchen garden without the constant eyesore of its formalities or the yearly nuisance of its decaying vegetation. Who can endure a cabbage bed in October?"

"Oh dear, yes. We are quite as well off for gardenstuff as ever we were; for if it is forgot to be brought at any time, we can always buy what we want at Sanditon House. The gardener there is glad enough to supply us. But it was a nice place for the children to run about in. So shady in summer!"

"My dear, we shall have shade enough on the hill, and more than enough in the course of a very few years. The growth of my plantations is a general astonishment. In the meanwhile, we have the canvas awning which gives us the most complete comfort within doors. And you can get a parasol at Whitby's for little Mary at any time, or a large bonnet at Jebb's. And as for the boys, I must say I would rather them run about in the sunshine than not. I am sure we agree, my dear, in wishing our boys to be as hardy as possible."

"Yes indeed, I am sure we do. And I will get Mary a little parasol, which will make her as proud as can be. How grave she will walk about with it and fancy herself quite a little woman. Oh, I have not the smallest doubt of our being a great deal better off where we are now. If we any of us want to bathe, we have not a quarter of a mile to go. But you know," still looking back, "one loves to look at an old friend, at a place where one has been happy. The Milliers did not seem to feel the storms last winter at all. I remember seeing Mrs. Millier after one of those dreadful nights, when we had been literally rocked in our bed, and she did not seem at all aware of the wind being anything more than common."

"Yes, yes, that's likely enough. We have all the grandeur of the storm with less real danger because the wind, meeting with nothing to oppose or confine it around our house, simply rages and passes on while down in this gutter. Nothing is known of the state of the air below the tops of the trees and the inhabitants may be taken totally unawares by one of those dreadful currents which do more mischief in a valley when they do arise than an open country ever experiences in the heaviest gale. But, my dear love, as to gardenstuff, you were saying that any accidental omission is supplied in a moment by Lady Denham's gardener. But it occurs to me that we ought to go elsewhere upon such occasions, and that old Stringer and his son have a higher claim. I encouraged him to set up, you know, and am afraid he does not do very well. That is, there has not been time enough yet. He will do very well beyond a doubt. But at first it is uphill work, and therefore we must give him what help we can. When any vegetables or fruit happen to be wanted, and it will not be amiss to have them often wanted, to have something or other forgotten most days, just to have a nominal supply, you know, that poor old Andrew may not lose his daily job, but in fact to buy the chief of our consumption from the Stringers."

"Very well, my love, that can be easily done. And cook will be satisfied, which will be a great comfort, for she is always complaining of old Andrew now and says he never brings her what she wants. There, now the old house is quite left behind. What is it your brother Sidney says about its being a hospital?"

"Oh, my dear Mary, merely a joke of his. He pretends to advise me to make a hospital of it. He pretends to laugh at my improvements. Sidney says anything, you know. He has always said what he chose of and to us all. Most families have such a member among them, I believe, Miss Heywood. There is someone in most families privileged by superior abilities or spirits to say anything. In ours it is Sidney, who is a very clever young man and with great powers of pleasing. He lives too much in the world to be settled, that is his only fault. He is here and there and everywhere. I wish we may get him to Sanditon. I should like to have you acquainted with him. And it would be a fine thing for the place! Such a young man as Sidney, with his neat equipage and fashionable air. You and I, Mary, know what effect it might have. Many a respectable family, many a careful mother, many a pretty daughter might it secure us to the prejudice of Eastbourne and Hastings."

They were now approaching the church and neat village of old Sanditon, which stood at the foot of the hill they were afterward to ascend. A hill whose side was covered with the woods and enclosures of Sanditon House and whose height ended in an open down where the new buildings might soon be looked for. A branch only of the valley, winding more obliquely toward the sea, gave a passage to an inconsiderable stream, and formed at its mouth a third habitable division in a small cluster of fishermen's houses.

The original village contained little more than cottages but the spirit of the day had been caught, as Mr. Parker observed with delight to Charlotte, and two or three of the best of them were smartened up with a white curtain and "Lodgings To Let"; and farther on, in the little green court of an old farmhouse, two females in elegant white were actually to be seen with their books and campstools and, in turning the corner of the baker's shop, the sound of a harp might be heard through the upper casement. Such sights and sounds were highly blissful to Mr. Parker. Not that he had any personal concern in the success of the village itself for, considering it as too remote from the beach, he had done nothing there. But it was a most valuable proof of the increasing fashion of the place altogether. If the village could attract, the hill might be nearly full. He anticipated an amazing season. At the same time last year (late in July), there had not been a single lodger in the village! Nor did he remember any during the whole summer, excepting one family of children who came from London for sea air after the whooping cough, and whose mother would not let them be nearer the shore for fear of their tumbling in.

"Civilization, civilization indeed!" cried Mr. Parker delighted. "Look, my dear Mary, look at William Heeley's windows. Blue shoes and nankeen boots! Who would have expected such a sight at a shoemaker's in old Sanditon! This is new within the month. There was no blue shoe when we passed this way a month ago.

Glorious indeed! Well, I think I have done something in my day. Now for our hill, our health-breathing hill."

In ascending, they passed the lodge gates of Sanditon House and saw the top of the house itself among its groves. It was the last building of former days in that line of the parish. A little higher up the modern began and in crossing the down, a Prospect House, a Bellevue Cottage, and a Denham Place were to be looked at by Charlotte with the calmness of amused curiosity and by Mr. Parker with the eager eye which hoped to see scarcely any empty houses. More bills at the windows than he had calculated on and a smaller show of company on the hill, fewer carriages, fewer walkers. He had fancied it just the time of day for them to be all returning from their airings to dinner but the sands and the Terrace always attracted some, and the tide must be flowing, about half-tide now. He longed to be on the sands, the cliffs, at his own house, and everywhere out of his house at once. His spirits rose with the very sight of the sea and he could almost feel his ankle getting stronger already.

Trafalgar House, on the most elevated spot on the down, was a light, elegant building, standing in a small lawn with a very young plantation round it, about a hundred yards from the brow of a steep but not very lofty cliff, and the nearest to it of every building, excepting one short row of smart-looking houses called the Terrace, with a broad walk in front, aspiring to be the Mall of the place. In this row were the best milliner's shop and the library, a little detached from it, the hotel and billiard room. Here began the descent to the beach and to the bathing machines. And this was therefore the favorite spot for beauty and fashion. At Trafalgar House, rising at a little distance behind the Terrace, the travelers were safely set down and all was happiness and joy between Papa and Mama and their children, while Charlotte, having received possession of her apartment, found amusement enough in standing at her ample Venetian window and looking over the miscellaneous foreground of unfinished buildings, waving linen and tops of houses, to the sea, dancing and sparkling in sunshine and freshness.

Chapter 5

When they met before dinner Mr. Parker was looking over letters. "Not a line from Sidney!" said he. "He is an idle fellow. I sent him an account of my accident from Willingden and thought he would have vouchsafed me an answer. But perhaps it implies that he is coming himself. I trust it may. But here is a letter from one of my sisters. They never fail me. Women are the only correspondents to be depended on. Now Mary," smiling at his wife, "before I open it, what shall we guess as to the state of health of those it comes from? Or rather, what would Sidney say if he were here? Sidney is a saucy fellow, Miss Heywood. And you must know, he will have it there is a good deal of imagination in my two sisters' complaints. But it really is not so, or very little. They have wretched health, as you have heard us say frequently, and are subject to a variety of very serious disorders. Indeed, I do not believe they know what a day's health is. And at the same time, they are such excellent useful women and have so much energy of character that where any good is to be done, they force themselves on exertions which, to those who do not thoroughly know them, have an extraordinary appearance. But there is really no affectation about them, you know. They have only weaker constitutions and stronger minds than are often met with, either separate or together. And our youngest brother, who lives with them and who is not much above twenty, I am sorry to say, is almost as great an invalid as themselves. He is so delicate that he can engage in no profession. Sidney laughs at him. But it really is no joke, though Sidney often makes me laugh at them all in spite of myself. Now, if he were here, I know he would be offering odds that either Susan, Diana, or Arthur would appear by this letter to have been at the point of death within the last month."

Having run his eye over the letter, he shook his head and began, "No chance of seeing them at Sanditon I am sorry to say. A very indifferent account of them indeed. Seriously, a very indifferent account. Mary, you will be quite sorry to hear how ill they have been and are. Miss Heywood, if you will give me leave, I will read Diana's letter aloud. I like to have my friends acquainted with each other and I am afraid this is the only sort of acquaintance I shall have the means of accomplishing between you. And I can have no scruple on Diana's account, for her letters show her exactly as she is, the most active, friendly, warmhearted being in existence, and therefore must give a good impression."

He read:

My dear Tom, we were all much grieved at your accident, and if you had not described yourself as fallen into such very good hands, I should have been with you, at all hazards, the day after the receipt of your letter, though it found me suffering under a more severe attack than usual of my old grievance, spasmodic bile, and hardly able to crawl from my bed to the sofa. But how were you treated? Send me more particulars in your next. If indeed a simple sprain, as you denominate it, nothing would have been so judicious as friction, friction by the hand alone, supposing it could be applied instantly. Two years ago I happened to be calling on Mrs. Sheldon when her coachman sprained his foot as he was cleaning the carriage and could hardly limp into the house, but by the immediate use of friction alone steadily persevered in (I rubbed his ankle with my own hand for six hours without intermission) he was well in three days. Many thanks, my dear Tom, for the kindness with respect to us, which had so large a share in bringing on your accident. But pray never run into peril again in looking for an apothecary on our account, for had you the most experienced man in his line settled at Sanditon, it would be no recommendation to us.

We have entirely done with the whole medical tribe. We have consulted physician after physician in vain, till we are quite convinced that they can do nothing for us and that we must trust to our own knowledge of our own wretched constitutions for any relief. But if you think it advisable for the interest of the place to get a medical man there, I will undertake the commission with pleasure, and have no doubt of succeeding. I could soon put the necessary irons in the fire. As for getting to Sanditon myself, it is quite an impossibility. I grieve to say that I dare not attempt it but my feelings tell me too plainly that, in my present state, the sea air would probably be the death of me. And neither of my dear companions will leave me or I would promote their going down to you for a fortnight. But in truth, I doubt whether Susan's nerves would be equal to the effort. She has been suffering much from the headache and six leeches a day for ten days together relieved her so little that we thought it right to change our measures, and being convinced, on examination, that much of the evil lay in her gum, I persuaded her to attack the disorder there. She has accordingly had three teeth drawn, and is decidedly better, but her nerves are a good deal deranged. She can only speak in a whisper and fainted away twice this morning on poor Arthur's trying to suppress a cough. He, I am happy to say, is tolerably well though more languid than I like and I fear for his liver. I have heard nothing of Sidney since your being together in town, but conclude his scheme to the Isle of Wight has not taken place or we should have seen him in his way. Most sincerely do we wish you a good season at Sanditon, and though we cannot contribute to your beau monde in person, we are doing our utmost to send you company worth having and think we may safely reckon on securing you two large families. One a rich West Indian from Surrey; the other a most respectable Girls Boarding School, or Academy, from Camberwell. I will not tell you how many people I have employed in the business, wheel within wheel. But success more than repays. Yours most affectionately, etcetera.

"Well," said Mr. Parker, as he finished. "Though I daresay Sidney might find something extremely entertaining in this letter and make us laugh for half an hour together, I declare I, by myself, can see nothing in it but what is either very pitiable or very creditable.

With all their sufferings you perceive how much they are occupied in promoting the good of others! So anxious for Sanditon! Two large families, one for Prospect House probably, the other for number two Denham Place or the end house of the Terrace, with extra beds at the hotel. I told you my sisters were excellent women, Miss Heywood."

"And I am sure they must be very extraordinary ones," said Charlotte. "I am astonished at the cheerful style of the letter, considering the state in which both sisters appear to be. Three teeth drawn at once. Frightful! Your sister Diana seems almost as ill as possible, but those three teeth of your sister Susan's are more distressing than all the rest."

"Oh, they are so used to the operation, to every operation, and have such fortitude!"

"Your sisters know what they are about, I daresay, but their measures seem to touch on extremes. I feel that in any illness I should be so anxious for professional advice, so very little venturesome for myself or anybody I loved! But then, we have been so healthy a family that I can be no judge of what the habit of self-doctoring may do."

"Why to own the truth," said Mrs. Parker, "I do think the Miss Parkers carry it too far sometimes. And so do you, my love, you know. You often think they would be better if they would leave themselves more alone, and especially Arthur. I know you think it a great pity they should give him such a turn for being ill."

"Well, well, my dear Mary, I grant you, it is unfortunate for poor Arthur that at his time of life he should be encouraged to give way to indisposition. It is bad that he should be fancying himself too sickly for any profession and sit down at one and twenty, on the interest of his own little fortune, without any idea of attempting to improve it or of engaging in any occupation that may be of use to himself or others. But let us talk of pleasanter things. These two large families are just what we wanted. But here is something at hand pleasanter still, Morgan with his 'Dinner on table.'"

Chapter 6

The party were very soon moving after dinner. Mr. Parker could not be satisfied without an early visit to the library and the library subscription book and Charlotte was glad to see as much and as quickly as possible where all was new. They were out in the very quietest part of a watering-place day, when the important business of dinner or of sitting after dinner was going on in almost every inhabited lodging. Here and there might be seen a solitary elderly man, who was forced to move early and walk for health, but in general, it was a thorough pause of company.

It was emptiness and tranquillity on the Terrace, the cliffs, and the sands. The shops were deserted. The straw hats and pendant lace seemed left to their fate both within the house and without, and Mrs. Whitby at the library was sitting in her inner room, reading one of her own novels for want of employment. The list of subscribers was but commonplace. The Lady Denham, Miss Brereton, Mr. and Mrs. Parker, Sir Edward Denham and Miss Denham, whose names might be said to lead off the season, were followed by nothing better than: Mrs. Mathews, Miss Mathews, Miss E. Mathews, Miss H. Mathews; Dr. and Mrs. Brown; Mr. Richard Pratt, Lieutenant Smith R.N., Captain Little—Limehouse, Mrs. Jane Fisher, Miss Fisher, Miss Scroggs, Reverend Mr. Hanking, Mr. Beard—Solicitor, Grays Inn; Mrs. Davis and Miss Merryweather.

Mr. Parker could not but feel that the list was not only without distinction but also less numerous than he had hoped. It was but July, however, and August and September were the months. And besides, the promised large families from Surrey and Camberwell were an ever-ready consolation. Mrs. Whitby came forward without delay from her literary recess, delighted to see Mr. Parker, whose manners recommended him to everybody, and they were fully occupied in their various civilities and communications while Charlotte, having added her name to the list as the first offering to the success of the season, was busy in some immediate purchases for the further good of everybody as soon as Mrs. Whitby could be hurried down from her toilette, with all her glossy curls and smart trinkets, to wait on her.

The library, of course, afforded everything: all the useless things in the world that could not be done without and among so many pretty temptations, and with so much good will for Mr. Parker to encourage expenditure, Charlotte began to feel that she must check herself, or rather she reflected that at two and twenty there could be no excuse for her doing otherwise, and that it would not do for her to be spending all her money the very first evening. She took up a book. It happened to be a volume of Camilla. She had not Camilla's youth, and had no intention of having her distress so she turned from the drawers of rings and brooches, repressed further solicitation and paid for what she had bought.

For her particular gratification, they were then to take a turn on the cliff but as they quitted the library they were met by two ladies whose arrival made an alteration necessary: Lady Denham and Miss Brereton. They had been to Trafalgar House and been directed thence to the library and, though Lady Denham was a great deal too active to regard the walk of a mile as anything requiring rest, and talked of going home again directly, the Parkers knew that to be pressed into their house and obliged to take her tea with them would suit her best and therefore the stroll on the cliff gave way to an immediate return home.

"No, no," said Her Ladyship. "I will not have you hurry your tea on my account. I know you like your tea late. My early hours are not to put my neighbors to inconvenience. No, no, Miss Clara and I will get back to our own tea. We came out with no other thought. We wanted just to see you and make sure of your being really come, but we get back to our own tea."

She went on, however, toward Trafalgar House and took possession of the drawing room very quietly without seeming to hear a word of Mrs. Parker's orders to the servant, as they entered, to bring tea directly. Charlotte was fully consoled for the loss of her walk by finding herself in company with those whom the conversation of the morning had given her a great curiosity to see. She observed them well. Lady Denham was of middle height, stout, upright and alert in her motions, with a shrewd eye and self-satisfied air but not an unagreeable countenance. And though her manner was rather downright and abrupt, as of a person who valued herself on being free-spoken, there was a good humor and cordiality about her, a civility and readiness to be acquainted with Charlotte herself and a heartiness of welcome toward her old friends which was inspiring the goodwill she seemed to feel.

And as for Miss Brereton, her appearance so completely justified Mr. Parker's praise that Charlotte thought she had never beheld a more lovely or more interesting young woman. Elegantly tall, regularly handsome, with great delicacy of complexion and soft blue eyes, a sweetly modest and yet naturally graceful address, Charlotte could see in her only the most perfect representation of whatever heroine might be most beautiful and bewitching in all the numerous volumes they had left behind on Mrs. Whitby's shelves. Perhaps it might be partly owing to her having just issued from a circulating library but she could not separate the idea of a complete heroine from Clara Brereton. Her situation with Lady Denham so very much in favor of it! She seemed placed with her on purpose to be ill-used. Such poverty and dependence joined to such beauty and merit seemed to leave no choice in the business. These feelings were not the result of any spirit of romance in Charlotte herself. No, she was a very sober-minded young lady, sufficiently well-read in novels to supply her imagination with amusement, but not at all unreasonably influenced by them, and while she pleased herself the first five minutes with fancying the persecution which ought to be the lot of the interesting Clara, especially in the form of the most barbarous conduct on Lady

Denham's side, she found no reluctance to admit from subsequent observation that they appeared to be on very comfortable terms. She could see nothing worse in Lady Denham than the sort of old-fashioned formality of always calling her Miss Clara, nor anything objectionable in the degree of observance and attention which Clara paid. On one side it seemed protecting kindness, on the other grateful and affectionate respect.

The conversation turned entirely upon Sanditon, its present number of visitants and the chances of a good season. It was evident that Lady Denham had more anxiety, more fears of loss, than her coadjutor. She wanted to have the place fill faster and seemed to have many harassing apprehensions of the lodgings being, in some instances, underlet. Miss Diana Parker's two large families were not forgotten.

"Very good, very good," said Her Ladyship. "A West Indy family and a school. That sounds well. That will bring money."

"No people spend more freely, I believe, than West Indians," observed Mr. Parker.

"Aye, so I have heard and because they have full purses fancy themselves equal, maybe, to your old country families. But then, they who scatter their money so freely never think of whether they may not be doing mischief by raising the price of things. And I have heard that's very much the case with your West Indians. And if they come among us to raise the price of our necessaries of life, we shall not much thank them, Mr. Parker."

"My dear Madam, they can only raise the price of consumable articles by such an extraordinary demand for them and such a diffusion of money among us as must do us more good than harm. Our butchers and bakers and traders in general cannot get rich without bringing prosperity to us. If they do not gain, our rents must be insecure and in proportion to their profit must be ours eventually in the increased value of our houses."

"Oh well! But I should not like to have butcher's meat raised though. And I shall keep it down as long as I can. Aye, that young lady smiles, I see. I daresay she thinks me an odd sort of creature but she will come to care about such matters herself in time. Yes, yes, my dear, depend upon it, you will be thinking of the price of butcher's meat in time, though you may not happen to have quite such a servants' hall to feed as I have. And I do believe those are best off that have fewest servants. I am not a woman of parade, as all the world knows, and if it was not for what I owe to poor Mr. Hollis's memory, I should never keep up Sanditon House as I do. It is not for my own pleasure. Well, Mr. Parker, and the other is a boarding school, a French boarding school, is it? No harm in that. They'll stay their six weeks. And out of such a number who knows? But some may be consumptive and want asses' milk and I have two milch asses at this present time. But perhaps the little Misses may hurt the furniture. I hope they will have a good sharp governess to look after them."

Poor Mr. Parker got no more credit from Lady Denham than he had from his sisters for the object that had taken him to Willingden.

"Lord! My dear Sir," she cried. "How could you think of such a thing? I am very sorry you met with your accident but, upon my word, you deserved it. Going after a doctor! Why, what should we do with a doctor here? It would be only encouraging our servants and the poor to fancy themselves ill if there was a doctor at hand. Oh! Pray, let us have none of the tribe at Sanditon. We go on very well as we are. There is the sea and the downs and my milch asses. And I have told Mrs. Whitby that if anybody inquires for a chamber-horse, they may be supplied at a fair rate. Poor Mr. Hollis's chamber-horse, as good as new and what can people want for more? Here have I lived seventy good years in the world and never took physic above twice and never saw the face of a doctor in all my life on my own account. And I verily believe if my poor dear Sir Harry had never seen one neither, he would have been alive now. Ten fees, one after another, did the man take who sent him out of the world. I beseech you, Mr. Parker, no doctors here."

The tea things were brought in. "Oh, my dear Mrs. Parker, you should not indeed. Why would you do so? I was just upon the point of wishing you good evening. But since you are so very neighborly, I believe Miss Clara and I must stay."

CHAPTER 7

The popularity of the Parkers brought them some visitors the very next morning. Amongst them Sir Edward Denham and his sister who, having been at Sanditon House, drove on to pay their compliments and, the duty of letter writing being accomplished, Charlotte was settled with Mrs. Parker in the drawing room in time to see them all. The Denhams were the only ones to excite particular attention. Charlotte was glad to complete her knowledge of the family by an introduction to them and found them, the better half at least (for while single, the gentleman may sometimes be thought the better half of the pair) not unworthy of notice. Miss Denham was a fine young woman but cold and reserved, giving the idea of one who felt her consequence with pride and her poverty with discontent, and who was immediately gnawed by the want of a handsomer equipage than the simple gig in which they traveled and which their groom was leading about still in her sight.

Sir Edward was much her superior in air and manner, certainly handsome, but yet more to be remarked for his very good address and wish of paying attention and giving pleasure. He came into the room remarkably well, talked much and very much to Charlotte by whom he chanced to be placed and she soon perceived that he had a fine countenance, a most pleasing gentleness of voice and a great deal of conversation. She liked him. Sober-minded as she was, she thought him agreeable and did not quarrel with the suspicion of his finding her equally so, which would arise from his evidently disregarding his sister's motion to go, and persisting in his station and his discourse.

I make no apologies for my heroine's vanity. If there are young ladies in the world at her time of life more dull of fancy and more careless of pleasing, I know them not and never wish to know them.

At last, from the low French windows of the drawing room which commanded the road and all the paths across the down, Charlotte and Sir Edward, as they sat, could not but observe Lady Denham and Miss Brereton walking by and there was instantly a slight change in Sir Edward's countenance. With an anxious glance after them as they proceeded, followed by an early proposal to his sister, not merely for moving, but for walking on together to the Terrace, which altogether gave a hasty turn to Charlotte's fancy, cured her of her half-hour's fever, and placed her in a more capable state of judging, when Sir Edward was gone, of how agreeable he had actually been. "Perhaps there was a good deal in his air and address and his title did him no harm." She was very soon in his company again.

The first object of the Parkers, when their house was cleared of morning visitors, was to get out themselves. The Terrace was the attraction to all. Everybody who walked must begin with the Terrace and there, seated on one of the two green benches by the gravel walk, they found the united Denham party but though united in the gross, very distinctly divided again: the two superior ladies being at one end of the bench, and Sir Edward and Miss Brereton at the other. Charlotte's first glance told her that Sir Edward's air was that of a lover. There could be no doubt of his devotion to Clara. How Clara received it was less obvious, but she was inclined to think not very favorably; for though sitting thus apart with him (which probably she might not have been able to prevent), her air was calm and grave. That the young lady at the other end of the bench was doing penance was indubitable. The difference in Miss Denham's countenance, the change from Miss Denham sitting in cold grandeur in Mrs. Parker's drawing room, to be kept from silence by the efforts of others, to Miss Denham at Lady Denham's elbow, listening and talking with smiling attention or solicitous eagerness, was very striking and very amusing or very melancholy, just as satire or morality might prevail. Miss Denham's character was pretty well decided with Charlotte. Sir Edward's required longer observation. He surprised her by quitting Clara immediately on their all joining and agreeing to walk, and by addressing his attentions entirely to herself. Stationing himself close by her, he seemed to mean to detach her as much as possible from the rest of the party and to give her the whole of his conversation. He began, in a tone of great taste and feeling, to talk of the sea and the seashore and ran with energy through all the usual phrases employed in praise of their sublimity and descriptive of the undescribable emotions they excite in the mind of sensibility. The terrific grandeur of the ocean in a storm, its glass surface in a calm, its gulls and its samphire and the deep fathoms of its abysses, its quick vicissitudes, its direful deceptions, its mariners tempting it in sunshine and overwhelmed by the sudden tempest; all were eagerly and fluently touched. Rather commonplace perhaps, but doing very well from the lips of a handsome Sir Edward, and she could not but think him a man of feeling, till he began to stagger her by the number of his quotations and the bewilderment of some of his sentences.

"Do you remember," said he, "Scott's beautiful lines on the sea? Oh! What a description they convey! They are never out of my thoughts when I walk here. That man who can read them unmoved must have the nerves of an assassin! Heaven defend me from meeting such a man unarmed."

"What description do you mean?" said Charlotte. "I remember none at this moment, of the sea, in either of Scott's poems."

"Do you not indeed? Nor can I exactly recall the beginning at this moment. But you cannot have forgotten his description of woman: 'Oh! Woman in our hours of ease.' Delicious! Delicious! Had he written nothing more, he would have been immortal. And then again, that unequaled, unrivaled address to parental affection, 'Some feelings are to mortals given with less of earth in them than heaven,' etcetera. But while we are on the subject of poetry, what think you, Miss Heywood, of Burns's lines to his Mary? Oh! There is pathos to madden one! If ever there was a man who felt, it was Burns. Montgomery has all the fire of poetry, Wordsworth has the true soul of it, Campbell, in his pleasures of hope, has touched the extreme of our sensations, 'Like angels' visits, few and far between.' Can you conceive anything more subduing, more melting, more fraught with the deep sublime than that line? But Burns, I confess my sense of his preeminence, Miss Heywood. If Scott has a fault, it is the want of passion. Tender, elegant, descriptive … but tame. The man who cannot do justice to the attributes of woman is my contempt. Sometimes indeed a flash of feeling seems to irradiate him, as in the lines we were speaking of, 'Oh! Woman in our hours of ease.' But Burns is always on fire. His soul was the altar in which lovely woman sat enshrined, his spirit truly breathed the immortal incense which is her due."

"I have read several of Burns's poems with great delight," said Charlotte as soon as she had time to speak. "But I am not poetic enough to separate a man's poetry entirely from his character and poor Burns's known irregularities greatly interrupt my enjoyment of his lines. I have difficulty in depending on the truth of his feelings as a lover. I have not faith in the sincerity of the affections of a man of his description. He felt and he wrote and he forgot."

"Oh! No, no," exclaimed Sir Edward in an ecstasy. "He was all ardor and truth! His genius and his susceptibilities might lead him into some aberrations. But who is perfect? It were hypercriticism, it were pseudo-philosophy to expect from the soul of high-toned genius the grovelings of a common mind. The coruscations of talent, elicited by impassioned feeling in the breast of man, are perhaps incompatible with some of the prosaic decencies of life; nor can you, loveliest Miss Heywood," speaking with an air of deep sentiment, "nor can any woman be a fair judge of what a man may be propelled to say, write, or do by the sovereign impulses of illimitable ardor."

This was very fine but if Charlotte understood it at all, not very moral, and being moreover by no means pleased with his extraordinary style of compliment, she gravely answered, "I really know nothing of the matter. This is a charming day. The wind, I fancy, must be southerly."

"Happy, happy wind, to engage Miss Heywood's thoughts!"

She began to think him downright silly. His choosing to walk with her she had learned to understand. It was done to pique Miss Brereton. She had read it, in an anxious glance or two on his side. But why he should talk so much nonsense, unless he could do no better, was unintelligible. He seemed very sentimental, very full of some feeling or other, and very much addicted to all the newest-fashioned hard words, had not a very clear brain, she presumed, and talked a good deal by rote. The future might explain him further. But when there was a proposition for going into the library, she felt that she had had quite enough of Sir Edward for one morning and very gladly accepted Lady Denham's invitation of remaining on the Terrace with her.

The others all left them, Sir Edward, with looks of very gallant despair in tearing himself away, and they united their agreeableness. That is, Lady Denham, like a true great lady, talked and talked only of her own concerns, and Charlotte listened, amused in considering the contrast between her two companions. Certainly there was no strain of doubtful sentiment nor any phrase of difficult interpretation in Lady Denham's discourse. Taking hold of Charlotte's arm with the ease of one who felt that any notice from her was an honor, and communicative from the influence of the same conscious importance or a natural love of talking, she immediately said in a tone of great satisfaction and with a look of arch sagacity, "Miss Esther wants me to invite her and her brother to spend a week with me at Sanditon House, as I did last summer. But I shan't. She has been trying to get round me every way with her praise of this and her praise of that but I saw what she was about. I saw through it all. I am not very easily taken in, my dear."

Charlotte could think of nothing more harmless to be said than the simple inquiry of, "Sir Edward and Miss Denham?"

"Yes, my dear. My young folks, as I call them sometimes, for I take them very much by the hand. I had them with me last summer, about this time, for a week. From Monday to Monday, and very delighted and thankful they were. For they are very good young people, my dear. I would not have you think that I only notice them for poor dear Sir Harry's sake. No, no! They are very deserving themselves or, trust me, they would not be so much in my company. I am not the woman to help anybody blindfold. I always take care to know what I am about and who I have to deal with before I stir a finger. I do not think I was ever overreached in my life. And that is a good deal for a woman to say that has been married twice. Poor dear Sir Harry, between ourselves, thought at first to have got more. But, with a bit of a sigh, he is gone, and we must not find fault with the dead. Nobody could live happier together than us, and he was a very honorable man, quite the gentleman of ancient family. And when he died, I gave Sir Edward his gold watch." She said this with a look at her companion that implied its right to produce a great impression and seeing no rapturous astonishment in Charlotte's countenance, added quickly, "He did not bequeath it to his nephew, my dear. It was no bequest. It was not in the will. He only told me, and that but once, that he should wish his nephew to have his watch but it need not have been binding if I had not chose it."

"Very kind indeed! Very handsome!" said Charlotte, absolutely forced to affect admiration.

"Yes, my dear, and it is not the only kind thing I have done by him. I have been a very liberal friend to Sir Edward. And poor young man, he needs it bad enough. For though I am only the dowager, my dear, and he is the heir, things do not stand between us in the way they commonly do between those two parties. Not a shilling do I receive from the Denham estate. Sir Edward has no payments to make me. He doesn't stand uppermost, believe me. It is I that help him."

"Indeed! He is a very fine young man, particularly elegant in his address." This was said chiefly for the sake of saying something, but Charlotte directly saw that it was laying her open to suspicion by Lady Denham's giving a shrewd glance at her and replying, "Yes, yes, he is very well to look at. And it is to be hoped that some lady of large fortune will think so, for Sir Edward must marry for money. He and I often talk that matter over. A handsome young fellow like him will go smirking and smiling about and paying girls compliments, but he knows he must marry for money. And Sir Edward is a very steady young man in the main and has got very good notions."

"Sir Edward Denham," said Charlotte, "with such personal advantages may be almost sure of getting a woman of fortune, if he chooses it." This glorious sentiment seemed quite to remove suspicion.

"Aye, my dear, that's very sensibly said," cried Lady Denham. "And if we could but get a young heiress to Sanditon! But heiresses are monstrous scarce! I do not think we have had an heiress here, or even a co since Sanditon has been a public place. Families come after families but, as far as I can learn, it is not one in a hundred of them that have any real property, landed or funded. An income perhaps, but no property. Clergymen maybe, or lawyers from town, or half-pay officers, or widows with only a jointure. And what good can such people do anybody? Except just as they take our empty houses and, between ourselves, I think they are great fools for not staying at home. Now if we could get a young heiress to be sent here for her health, and if she was ordered to drink asses' milk I could supply her and, as soon as she got well, have her fall in love with Sir Edward!"

"That would be very fortunate indeed."

"And Miss Esther must marry somebody of fortune, too. She must get a rich husband. Ah, young ladies that have no money are very much to be pitied! But," after a short pause, "if Miss Esther thinks to talk me into inviting them to come and stay at Sanditon House, she will find herself mistaken. Matters are altered with me since last summer, you know. I have Miss Clara with me now which makes a great difference." She spoke this so seriously that Charlotte instantly saw in it the evidence of real penetration and prepared for some fuller remarks but it was followed only by, "I have no fancy for having my house as full as an hotel. I should not choose to have my two housemaids' time taken up all the morning in dusting out bedrooms. They have Miss Clara's room to put to rights as well as my own every day. If they had hard places, they would want higher wages." For objections of this nature, Charlotte was not prepared. She found it so impossible even to affect sympathy that she could say nothing. Lady Denham soon added, with great glee, "And besides all this, my dear, am I to be filling my house to the prejudice of Sanditon? If people want to be by the sea, why don't they take lodgings? Here are a great many empty houses, three on this very Terrace. No fewer than three lodging papers staring me in the face at this very moment; numbers three, four, and eight. Eight, the corner house, may be too large for them, but either of the two others are nice little snug houses, very fit for a young gentleman and his sister. And so, my dear, the next time Miss Esther begins talking about the dampness of Denham Park and the good bathing always does her, I shall advise them to come and take one of these lodgings for a fortnight. Don't you think that will be very fair? Charity begins at home, you know."

Charlotte's feelings were divided between amusement and indignation, but indignation had the larger and the increasing share. She kept her countenance and she kept a civil silence. She could not carry her forbearance farther, but without attempting to listen longer, and only conscious that Lady Denham was still talking on in the same way, allowed her thoughts to form themselves into such a meditation as this: "She is thoroughly mean. I had not expected anything so bad, Mr. Parker spoke too mildly of her. His judgment is evidently not to be trusted. His own good nature misleads him. He is too kindhearted to see clearly. I must judge for myself. And their very connection prejudices him. He has persuaded her to engage in the same speculation, and because their object in that line is the same, he fancies she feels like him in others. But she is very, very mean. I can see no good in her. Poor Miss Brereton! And she makes everybody mean about her. This poor Sir Edward and his sister! How far nature meant them to be respectable I cannot tell but they are obliged to be mean in their servility to her. And I am mean, too, in giving her my attention with the appearance of coinciding with her. Thus it is, when rich people are sordid."

The two ladies continued walking together till, rejoined by the others, who, as they issued from the library, were followed by a young Whitby running off with five volumes under his arm to Sir Edward's gig and Sir Edward, approaching Charlotte, said, "You may perceive what has been our occupation. My sister wanted my counsel in the selection of some books. We have many leisure hours and read a great deal. I am no indiscriminate novel reader. The mere trash of the common circulating library I hold in the highest contempt. You will never hear me advocating those puerile emanations which detail nothing but discordant principles incapable of amalgamation, or those vapid tissues of ordinary occurrences from which no useful deductions can be drawn. In vain may we put them into a literary alembic. We distill nothing that can add to science. You understand me, I am sure?"

"I am not quite certain that I do. But if you will describe the sort of novels which you do approve, I daresay it will give me a clearer idea."

"Most willingly, fair questioner. The novels which I approve are such as display human nature with grandeur; such as show her in the sublimities of intense feeling, such as exhibit the progress of strong passion from the first germ of incipient susceptibility to the utmost energies of reason half-dethroned, where we see the strong spark of woman's captivations elicit such fire in the soul of man as leads him, though at the risk of some aberration from the strict line of primitive obligations, to hazard all, dare all, achieve all to obtain her. Such are the works which I peruse with delight and, I hope I may say, with amelioration. They hold forth the most splendid portraitures of high conceptions, unbounded views, illimitable ardor, indomitable decision. And even when the event is mainly anti-prosperous to the high-toned machinations of the prime character the potent, pervading hero of the story, it leaves us full of generous emotions for him; our hearts are paralyzed. It would be pseudo-philosophy to assert that we do not feel more enwrapped by the brilliancy of his career than by the tranquil and morbid virtues of any opposing character. Our approbation of the latter is but eleemosynary. These are the novels which enlarge the primitive capabilities of the heart and it cannot impugn the sense or be any dereliction of the character of the most anti-puerile man, to be conversant with them.

"If I understand you aright," said Charlotte, "our taste in novels is not at all the same." And here they were obliged to part, Miss Denham being much too tired of them all to stay any longer. The truth was that Sir Edward, who circumstances had confined very much to one spot, had read more sentimental novels than agreed with him. His fancy had been early caught by all the impassioned and most exceptionable parts of Richardson's. And such authors as had since appeared to tread in Richardson's steps (so far as man's determined pursuit of woman in defiance of every opposition of feeling and convenience was concerned) had since occupied the greater part of his literary hours, and formed his character. With a perversity of judgment that must be attributed to his not having by nature a very strong head, the graces, the spirit, the sagacity, and the perseverance of the villain of the story outweighed all his absurdities and all his atrocities with Sir Edward. With him such conduct was genius, fire, and feeling. It interested and inflamed him. And he was always more anxious for its success, and mourned over its discomfitures with more tenderness, than could ever have been contemplated by the authors. Though he owed many of his ideas to this sort of reading, it would be unjust to say that he read nothing else or that his language was not formed on a more general knowledge of modern literature. He read all the essays, letters, tours, and criticisms of the day; and with the same ill-luck which made him derive only false principles from lessons of morality, and incentives to vice from the history of its overthrow, he gathered only hard words and involved sentences from the style of our most approved writers.

Sir Edward's great object in life was to be seductive. With such personal advantages as he knew himself to possess, and such talents as he did also give himself credit for, he regarded it as his duty. He felt that he was affirmed to be a dangerous man, quite in the line of the Lovelaces. The very name of Sir Edward, he thought, carried some degree of fascination with it. To be generally gallant and assiduous about the fair, to make fine speeches to every pretty girl, was but the inferior part of the character he had to play. Miss Heywood, or any other young woman with any pretensions to beauty, he was entitled, according to his own views of society, to approach with high compliment and rhapsody on the slightest acquaintance.

But it was Clara alone on whom he had serious designs. It was Clara whom he meant to seduce. Her seduction was quite determined on. Her situation in every way called for it. She was his rival in Lady Denham's favor, she was young, lovely, and dependent. He had very early seen the necessity of the case, and had now been long trying with cautious assiduity to make an impression on her heart and to undermine her principles. Clara saw through him and had not the least intention of being seduced but she bore with him patiently enough to confirm the sort of attachment that her personal charms had raised. A greater degree of discouragement indeed would not have affected Sir Edward. He was armed against the highest pitch of disdain or aversion. If she could not be won by affection, he must carry her off. He knew his business. Already had he had many musings on the subject. If he were constrained so to act, he must naturally wish to strike out something new, to exceed those who had gone before him and he felt a strong curiosity to ascertain whether the neighborhood of Timbuktu might not afford some solitary house adapted for Clara's reception. But the expense, alas! of measures in that masterly style was ill-suited to his purse and prudence obliged him to prefer the quietest sort of ruin and disgrace for the object of his affections to the more renowned.

Chapter 8

One day, soon after Charlotte's arrival at Sanditon she had the pleasure of seeing, just as she ascended from the sands to the Terrace, a gentleman's carriage with post horses standing at the door of the hotel, as very lately arrived and by the quantity of luggage being taken off bringing, it might be hoped, some respectable family determined on a long residence. Delighted to have such good news for Mr. and Mrs. Parker, who had both gone home some time before, she proceeded to Trafalgar House with as much alacrity as could remain after having contended for the last two hours with a very fine wind blowing directly onshore.

But she had not reached the little lawn when she saw a lady walking nimbly behind her at no great distance and, convinced that it could be no acquaintance of her own, she resolved to hurry on and get into the house, if possible, before her. But the stranger's pace did not allow this to be accomplished. Charlotte was on the steps and had rung, but the door was not open when the other crossed the lawn and when the servant appeared, they were just equally ready for entering the house. The ease of the lady, her "How do you do, Morgan?" and Morgan's looks on seeing her were a moment's astonishment but another moment brought Mr. Parker into the hall to welcome the sister he had seen from the drawing room and Charlotte was soon introduced to Miss Diana Parker. There was a great deal of surprise but still more pleasure in seeing her. Nothing could be kinder than her reception from both husband and wife. How did she come? And with whom? And they were so glad to find her equal to the journey! And that she was to belong to them was taken as a matter of course.

Miss Diana Parker was about four and thirty, of middling height and slender, delicate looking rather than sickly with an agreeable face and a very animated eye, her manners resembling her brother's in their ease and frankness, though with more decision and less mildness in her tone. She began an account of herself without delay. Thanking them for their invitation but that was, "quite out of the question for they were all three come and meant to get into lodgings and make some stay."

"All three come! What! Susan and Arthur! Susan able to come too!" This was better and better.

"Yes, we are actually all come. Cite unavoidable. Nothing else to be done. You shall hear all about it. But my dear Mary, send for the children. I long to see them."

"And how has Susan borne the journey? And how is Arthur? And why do we not see him here with you?"

"Susan has borne it wonderfully. She had not a wink of sleep either the night before we set out or last night at Chichester, and, as this is not so common with her as with me, I have had a thousand fears for her. But she has kept up wonderfully, no hysterics of consequence till we came within sight of poor old Sanditon and the attack was not very violent, nearly over by the time we reached your hotel so that we got her out of the carriage extremely well with only Mr. Woodcock's assistance. And when I left her she was directing the disposal of the luggage and helping old Sam uncord the trunks. She desired her best love with a thousand regrets at being so poor a creature that she could not come with me. And as for poor Arthur, he would not have been unwilling himself, but there is so much wind that I did not think he could safely venture, for I am sure there is lumbago hanging about him, and so I helped him on with his greatcoat and sent him off to the Terrace to take us lodgings. Miss Heywood must have seen our carriage standing at the hotel. I knew Miss Heywood the moment I saw her before me on the down. My dear Tom, I am so glad to see you walk so well. Let me feel your ankle. That's right. All right and clean. The play of your sinews a *very* little affected, barely perceptible. Well, now for the explanation of my being here. I told you in my letter of the two considerable families I was hoping to secure for you, the West Indians and the seminary."

Here Mr. Parker drew his chair still nearer to his sister and took her hand again most affectionately as he answered, "Yes, yes, how active and how kind you have been!"

"The West Indians," she continued, "whom I look upon as the most desirable of the two, as the best of the good, prove to be a Mrs. Griffiths and her family. I know them only through others. You must have heard me mention Miss Capper, the particular friend of my very particular friend Fanny Noyce. Now, Miss Capper is extremely intimate with a Mrs. Darling, who is on terms of constant correspondence with Mrs. Griffiths herself. Only a short chain, you see, between us, and not a link wanting. Mrs. Griffiths meant to go to the sea for her young people's benefit, had fixed on the coast of Sussex but was undecided as to the where, wanted something private, and wrote to ask the opinion of her friend Mrs. Darling. Miss Capper happened to be staying with Mrs. Darling when Mrs. Griffiths's letter arrived and was consulted on the question. She wrote the same day to Fanny Noyce and mentioned it to her and Fanny, all alive for us, instantly took up her pen and forwarded the circumstance to me, except as to names, which have but lately transpired. There was but one thing for me to do. I answered Fanny's letter by the same post and pressed for the recommendation of Sanditon. Fanny had feared your having no house large enough to receive such a family. But I seem to be spinning out my story to an endless length. You see how it was all managed. I had the pleasure of hearing soon afterward by the same simple link of connection that Sanditon had been recommended by Mrs. Darling, and that the West Indians were very much disposed to go thither. This was the state of the case when I wrote to you. But two days ago, yes, the day before yesterday I heard again from Fanny Noyce, saying that she had heard from Miss Capper, who by a letter from Mrs. Darling understood that Mrs. Griffiths had expressed herself in a letter to Mrs. Darling more doubtingly on the subject of Sanditon. Am I clear? I would be anything rather than not clear."

"Oh, perfectly, perfectly. Well?"

"The reason of this hesitation was her having no connections in the place, and no means of ascertaining that she should have good accommodations on arriving there and she was particularly careful and scrupulous on all those matters more on account of a certain Miss Lambe, a young lady, probably a niece, under her care than on her own account or her daughters. Miss Lambe has an immense fortune, richer than all the rest, and very delicate health. One sees clearly enough by all this the sort of woman Mrs. Griffiths must be, as helpless and indolent as wealth and a hot climate are apt to make us. But we are not born to equal energy. What was to be done? I had a few moments' indecision, whether to offer to write to you or to Mrs. Whitby to secure them a house but neither pleased me. I hate to employ others when I am equal to act myself and my conscience told me that this was an occasion that called for me. Here was a family of helpless invalids whom I might essentially serve. I sounded Susan. The same thought had occurred to her. Arthur made no difficulties. Our plan was arranged immediately, we were off yesterday morning at six, left Chichester at the same hour today … and here we are."

"Excellent! Excellent!" cried Mr. Parker. "Diana, you are unequaled in serving your friends and doing good to all the world. I know nobody like you. Mary, my love, is not she a wonderful creature? Well, and now, what house do you design to engage for them? What is the size of their family?"

"I do not at all know," replied his sister, "have not the least idea, never heard any particulars but I am very sure that the largest house at Sanditon cannot be too large. They are more likely to want a second. I shall take only one, however, and that but for a week certain. Miss Heywood, I astonish you. You hardly know what to make of me. I see by your looks that you are not used to such quick measures."

The words "unaccountable officiousness!" and "activity run mad!" had just passed through Charlotte's mind, but a civil answer was easy. "I daresay I do look surprised," said she, "because these are very great exertions, and I know what invalids both you and your sister are."

"Invalids, indeed. I trust there are not three people in England who have so sad a right to that appellation! But my dear Miss Heywood, we are sent into this world to be as extensively useful as possible, and where some degree of strength of mind is given, it is not a feeble body that will excuse us or incline us to excuse ourselves. The world is pretty much divided between the weak of mind and the strong; between those who can act and those who cannot; and it is the bounden duty of the capable to let no opportunity of being useful escape them. My sister's complaints and mine are, happily, not often of a nature to threaten existence immediately. And as long as we can exert ourselves to be of use to others, I am convinced that the body is the better for the refreshment the mind receives in doing its duty. While I have been traveling with this object in view, I have been perfectly well."

The entrance of the children ended this little panegyric on her own disposition and, after having noticed and caressed them all, she prepared to go.

"Cannot you dine with us? Is not it possible to prevail on you to dine with us?" was then the cry. And that being absolutely negatived, it was, "And when shall we see you again? And how can we be of use to you?" And Mr. Parker warmly offered his assistance in taking the house for Mrs. Griffiths. "I will come to you the moment I have dined," said he, "and we will go about together."

But this was immediately declined. "No, my dear Tom, upon no account in the world shall you stir a step on any business of mine. Your ankle wants rest. I see by the position of your foot that you have used it too much already. No, I shall go about my house-taking directly. Our dinner is not ordered till six and by that time I hope to have completed it. It is now only half past four. As to seeing me again today, I cannot answer for it. The others will be at the hotel all the evening and delighted to see you at any time but as soon as I get back I shall hear what Arthur has done about our own lodgings, and probably the moment dinner is over shall be out again on business relative to them, for we hope to get into some lodgings or other and be settled after breakfast tomorrow. I have not much confidence in poor Arthur's skill for lodging-taking, but he seemed to like the commission."

"I think you are doing too much," said Mr. Parker. "You will knock yourself out. You should not move again after dinner."

"No, indeed you should not," cried his wife, "for dinner is such a mere name with you all that it can do you no good. I know what your appetites are."

"My appetite is very much mended, I assure you, lately. I have been taking some bitters of my own decocting, which have done wonders. Susan never eats, I grant you and just at present I shall want nothing. I never eat for about a week after a journey. But as for Arthur, he is only too much disposed for food. We are often obliged to check him."

"But you have not told me anything of the other family coming to Sanditon," said Mr. Parker as he walked with her to the door of the house. "The Camberwell Seminary. Have we a good chance of them?"

"Oh, certain. Quite certain. I had forgotten them for the moment. But I had a letter three days ago from my friend Mrs. Charles Dupuis which assured me of Camberwell. Camberwell will be here to a certainty, and very soon. That good woman, I do not know her name, not being so wealthy and independent as Mrs. Griffiths, can travel and choose for herself. I will tell you how I got at her. Mrs. Charles Dupuis lives almost next door to a lady, who has a relation lately settled at Clapham, who actually attends the seminary and gives lessons on eloquence and *belles lettres* to some of the girls. I got this man a hare from one of Sidney's friends and he recommended Sanditon. Without my appearing however Mrs. Charles Dupuis managed it all."

CHAPTER 9

It was not a week since Miss Diana Parker had been told by her feelings that the sea air would probably, in her present state, be the death of her; and now she was at Sanditon, intending to make some stay and without appearing to have the slightest recollection of having written or felt any such thing. It was impossible for Charlotte not to suspect a good deal of fancy in such an extraordinary state of health. Disorders and recoveries so very much out of the common way seemed more like the amusement of eager minds in want of employment than of actual afflictions and relief.

The Parkers were no doubt a family of imagination and quick feelings, and while the eldest brother found vent for his superfluity of sensation as a projector, the sisters were perhaps driven to dissipate theirs in the invention of odd complaints. The whole of their mental vivacity was evidently not so employed, part was laid out in a zeal for being useful. It would seem that they must either be very busy for the good of others or else extremely ill themselves. Some natural delicacy of constitution, in fact, with an unfortunate turn for medicine, especially quack medicine, had given them an early tendency at various times to various disorders. The rest of their sufferings were from fancy, the love of distinction and the love of the wonderful. They had charitable hearts and many amiable feelings but a spirit of restless activity and the glory of doing more than anybody else had their share in every exertion of benevolence and there was vanity in all they did, as well as in all they endured.

Mr. and Mrs. Parker spent a great part of the evening at the hotel but Charlotte had only two or three views of Miss Diana posting over the down after a house for this lady whom she had never seen and who had never employed her. She was not made acquainted with the others till the following day when, being removed into lodgings and all the party continuing quite well, their brother and sister and herself were entreated to drink tea with them. They were in one of the Terrace houses and she found them arranged for the evening in a small neat drawing room with a beautiful view of the sea if they had chosen it. But though it had been a very fair English summer day, not only was there no open window, but the sofa and the table and the establishment in general was all at the other end of the room by a brisk fire. Miss Parker, whom, remembering the three teeth drawn in one day, Charlotte approached with a peculiar degree of respectful compassion, was not very unlike her sister in person or manner, though more thin and worn by illness and medicine, more relaxed in air and more subdued in voice. She talked, however, the whole evening as incessantly as Diana and, excepting that she sat with salts in her hand, took drops two or three times from one out of several vials already at home on the mantelpiece and made a great many odd faces and contortions, Charlotte could perceive no symptoms of illness which she, in the boldness of her own good health, would not have undertaken to cure by putting out the fire, opening the window, and disposing of the drops and the salts by means of one or the other.

She had had considerable curiosity to see Mr. Arthur Parker and having fancied him a very puny, delicate-looking young man, materially the smallest of a not very robust family, was astonished to find him quite as tall as his brother and a great deal stouter, broad made and lusty, and with no other look of an invalid than a sodden complexion. Diana was evidently the chief of the family, principal mover and actor. She had been on her feet the whole morning, on Mrs. Griffiths's business or their own, and was still the most alert of the three. Susan had only superintended their final removal from the hotel, bringing two heavy boxes herself, and Arthur had found the air so cold that he had merely walked from one house to the other as nimbly as he could, and boasted much of sitting by the fire till he had cooked up a very good one.

Diana, whose exercise had been too domestic to admit of calculation but who, by her own account, had not once sat down during the space of seven hours, confessed herself a little tired. She had been too successful, however, for much fatigue for not only had she, by walking and talking down a thousand difficulties, at last secured a proper house at eight guineas per week for Mrs. Griffiths, she had also opened so many treaties with cooks, housemaids, washerwomen, and bathing women that Mrs. Griffiths would have little more to do on her arrival than to wave her hand and collect them around her for choice. Her concluding effort in the cause had been a few polite lines of information to Mrs. Griffiths herself, time not allowing for the circuitous train of intelligence which had been hitherto kept up and she was now regaling in the delight of opening the first trenches of an acquaintance with such a powerful discharge of unexpected obligation.

Mr. and Mrs. Parker and Charlotte had seen two post chaises crossing the down to the hotel as they were setting off, a joyful sight and full of speculation. The Miss Parkers and Arthur had also seen something; they could distinguish from their window that there was an arrival at the hotel, but not its amount. Their visitors answered for two hack chaises. Could it be the Camberwell Seminary? No, no. Had there been a third carriage perhaps it might, but it was very generally agreed that two hack chaises could never contain a seminary. Mr. Parker was confident of another new family. When they were all finally seated, after some removals to look at the sea and the hotel, Charlotte's place was by Arthur, who was sitting next to the fire with a degree of enjoyment which gave a good deal of merit to his civility in wishing her to take his chair. There was nothing dubious in her manner of declining it and he sat down again with much satisfaction. She drew back her chair to have all the advantage of his person as a screen and was very thankful for every inch of back and shoulders beyond her preconceived idea. Arthur was heavy in eye as well as figure but by no means indisposed to talk and while the other four were chiefly engaged together, he evidently felt it no penance to have a fine young woman next to him, requiring, in common politeness, some attention, as his brother, who felt the decided want of some motive for action, some powerful object of animation for him, observed with considerable pleasure. Such was the influence of youth and bloom that he began even to make a sort of apology for having a fire.

"We should not have had one at home," said he, "but the sea air is always damp. I am not afraid of anything so much as damp."

"I am so fortunate," said Charlotte, "as never to know whether the air is damp or dry. It has always some property that is wholesome and invigorating to me."

"I like the air too, as well as anybody can," replied Arthur. "I am very fond of standing at an open window when there is no wind. But, unluckily, a damp air does not like me. It gives me the rheumatism. You are not rheumatic, I suppose?"

"Not at all."

"That's a great blessing. But perhaps you are nervous?"

"No, I believe not. I have no idea that I am."

"I am very nervous. To say the truth, nerves are the worst part of my complaints in my opinion. My sisters think me bilious, but I doubt it."

"You are quite in the right to doubt it as long as you possibly can, I am sure."

"If I were bilious," he continued, "you know, wine would disagree with me, but it always does me good. The more wine I drink, in moderation, the better I am. I am always best of an evening. If you had seen me today before dinner, you would have thought me a very poor creature."

Charlotte could believe it. She kept her countenance, however, and said, "As far as I can understand what nervous complaints are, I have a great idea of the efficacy of air and exercise for them, daily, regular exercise, and I should recommend rather more of it to you than I suspect you are in the habit of taking."

"Oh, I am very fond of exercise myself," he replied, "and I mean to walk a great deal while I am here, if the weather is temperate. I shall be out every morning before breakfast and take several turns upon the Terrace, and you will often see me at Trafalgar House."

"But you do not call a walk to Trafalgar House much exercise?"

"Not as to mere distance, but the hill is so steep! Walking up that hill, in the middle of the day, would throw me into such a perspiration! You would see me all in a bath by the time I got there! I am very subject to perspiration, and there cannot be a surer sign of nervousness."

They were now advancing so deep in physics that Charlotte viewed the entrance of the servant with the tea things as a very fortunate interruption. It produced a great and immediate change. The young man's attentions were instantly lost. He took his own cocoa from the tray, which seemed provided with almost as many teapots as there were persons in company, Miss Parker drinking one sort of herb tea and Miss Diana another, and turning completely to the fire, sat coddling and cooking it to his own satisfaction and toasting some slices of bread, brought up ready-prepared in the toast rack and till it was all done, she heard nothing of his voice but the murmuring of a few broken sentences of self-approbation and success. When his toils were over, however, he moved back his chair into as gallant a line as ever, and proved that he had not been working only for himself by his earnest invitation to her to take both cocoa and toast. She was already helped to tea, which surprised him, so totally self-engrossed had he been. "I thought I should have been in time," said he, "but cocoa takes a great deal of boiling."

"I am much obliged to you," replied Charlotte. "But I prefer tea."

"Then I will help myself," said he. "A large dish of rather weak cocoa every evening agrees with me better than anything."

It struck her, however, as he poured out this rather weak cocoa, that it came forth in a very fine, dark-colored stream and at the same moment, his sisters both crying out, "Oh, Arthur, you get your cocoa stronger and stronger every evening," with Arthur's somewhat conscious reply of "'Tis rather stronger than it should be tonight," convinced her that Arthur was by no means so fond of being starved as they could desire or as he felt proper himself. He was certainly very happy to turn the conversation on dry toast and hear no more of his sisters. "I hope you will eat some of this toast," said he. "I reckon myself a very good toaster. I never burn my toasts, I never put them too near the fire at first. And yet, you see, there is not a corner but what is well browned. I hope you like dry toast."

"With a reasonable quantity of butter spread over it, very much," said Charlotte, "but not otherwise."

"No more do I," said he, exceedingly pleased. "We think quite alike there. So far from dry toast being wholesome, I think it a very bad thing for the stomach. Without a little butter to soften it, it hurts the coats of the stomach. I am sure it does. I will have the pleasure of spreading some for you directly, and afterward I will spread some for myself. Very bad indeed for the coats of the stomach but there is no convincing some people. It irritates and acts like a nutmeg grater." He could not get command of the butter, however, without a struggle, his sisters accusing him of eating a great deal too much and declaring he was not to be trusted, and he maintaining that he only ate enough to secure the coats of his stomach, and besides, he only wanted it now for Miss Heywood. Such a plea must prevail. He got the butter and spread away for her with an accuracy of judgment which at least delighted himself. But when her toast was done and he took his own in hand, Charlotte could hardly contain herself as she saw him watching his sisters while he scrupulously scraped off almost as much butter as he put on, and then seizing an odd moment for adding a great dab just before it went into his mouth.

Certainly, Mr. Arthur Parker's enjoyments in invalidism were very different from his sisters, by no means so spiritualized. A good deal of earthy dross hung about him. Charlotte could not but suspect him of adopting that line of life principally for the indulgence of an indolent temper, and to be determined on having no disorders but such as called for warm rooms and good nourishment. In one particular, however, she soon found that he had caught something from them.

"What!" said he. "Do you venture upon two dishes of strong

green tea in one evening? What nerves you must have! How I envy you. Now, if I were to swallow only one such dish, what do you think its effect would be upon me?"

"Keep you awake perhaps all night," replied Charlotte, meaning to overthrow his attempts at surprise by the grandeur of her own conceptions.

"Oh, if that were all!" he exclaimed. "No. It acts on me like poison and would entirely take away the use of my right side before I had swallowed it five minutes. It sounds almost incredible, but it has happened to me so often that I cannot doubt it. The use of my right side is entirely taken away for several hours!"

"It sounds rather odd to be sure," answered Charlotte coolly, "but I daresay it would be proved to be the simplest thing in the world by those who have studied right sides and green tea scientifically and thoroughly understand all the possibilities of their action on each other."

Soon after tea, a letter was brought to Miss Diana Parker from the hotel. "From Mrs. Charles Dupuis," said she, "some private hand," and having read a few lines, exclaimed aloud, "Well, this is very extraordinary! Very extraordinary indeed! That both should have the same name. Two Mrs. Griffiths! This is a letter of recommendation and introduction to me of the lady from Camberwell and her name happens to be Griffiths too." A few more lines, however, and the color rushed into her cheeks and with much perturbation, she added, "The oddest thing that ever was! A Miss Lambe too! A young West Indian of large fortune. But it cannot be the same. Impossible that it should be the same."

She read the letter aloud for comfort. It was merely to introduce the bearer, Mrs. Griffiths from Camberwell, and the three young ladies under her care to Miss Diana Parker's notice. Mrs. Griffiths, being a stranger at Sanditon, was anxious for a respectable introduction; and Mrs. Charles Dupuis, therefore, at the instance of the intermediate friend, provided her with this letter, knowing that she could not do her dear Diana a greater kindness than by giving her the means of being useful. "Mrs. Griffiths's chief solicitude would be for the accommodation and comfort of one of the young ladies under her care, a Miss Lambe, a young West Indian of large fortune in delicate health," read Diana. It was very strange! Very remarkable! Very extraordinary! But they were all agreed in determining it to be impossible that there should not be two families; such a totally distinct set of people as were concerned in the reports of each made that matter quite certain. There must be two families. Impossible to be otherwise. "Impossible" and "Impossible" were repeated over and over again with great fervor. An accidental resemblance of names and circumstances, however striking at first, involved nothing really incredible and so it was settled. Miss Diana herself derived an immediate advantage to counterbalance her perplexity. She must put her shawl over her shoulders and be running about again. Tired as she was, she must instantly repair to the hotel to investigate the truth and offer her services.

CHAPTER 10

It would not do. Not all that the whole Parker race could say among themselves could produce a happier catastrophe than that the family from Surrey and the family from Camberwell were one and the same. The rich West Indians and the young ladies' seminary had all entered Sanditon in those two hack chaises. The Mrs. Griffiths who, in her friend Mrs. Darling's hands, had wavered as to coming and been unequal to the journey, was the very same Mrs. Griffiths whose plans were at the same period (under another representation) perfectly decided, and who was without fears or difficulties. All that had the appearance of incongruity in the reports of the two might very fairly be placed to the account of the vanity, the ignorance, or the blunders of the many engaged in the cause by the vigilance and caution of Miss Diana Parker. Her intimate friends must be officious like herself; and the subject had supplied letters and extracts and messages enough to make everything appear what it was not.

Miss Diana probably felt a little awkward on being first obliged to admit her mistake. A long journey from Hampshire taken for nothing, a brother disappointed, an expensive house on her hands for a week must have been some of her immediate reflections; and much worse than all the rest must have been the sensation of being less clear-sighted and infallible than she had believed herself. No part of it, however, seemed to trouble her for long. There were so many to share in the shame and the blame that probably, when she had divided out their proper portions to Mrs. Darling, Miss Capper, Fanny Noyce, Mrs. Charles Dupuis, and Mrs. Charles Dupuis's neighbor, there might be a mere trifle of reproach remaining for herself. At any rate, she was seen all the following morning walking about after lodgings with Mrs. Griffiths as alert as ever. Mrs. Griffiths was a very well-behaved, genteel kind of woman, who supported herself by receiving such great girls and young ladies as wanted either masters for finishing their education or a home for beginning their displays. She had several more under her care than the three who were now come to Sanditon, but the others all happened to be absent.

Of these three, and indeed of all, Miss Lambe was beyond comparison the most important and precious, as she paid in proportion to her fortune. She was about seventeen, half mulatto, chilly and tender, had a maid of her own, was to have the best room in the lodgings, and was always of the first consequence in every plan of Mrs. Griffiths. The other girls, two Miss Beauforts, were just such young ladies as may be met with in at least one family out of three throughout the kingdom. They had tolerable complexions, showy figures, an upright decided carriage, and an assured look; they were very accomplished and very ignorant, their time being divided between such pursuits as might attract admiration, and those labors and expedients of dexterous ingenuity by which they could dress in a style much beyond what they ought to have afforded; they were some of the first in every change of fashion. And the object of all was to captivate some man of much better fortune than their own.

Mrs. Griffiths had preferred a small, retired place like Sanditon on Miss Lambe's account and the Miss Beauforts, though naturally preferring anything to smallness and retirement, having in the course of the spring been involved in the inevitable expense of six new dresses each for a three-days visit, were constrained to be satisfied with Sanditon also till their circumstances were retrieved. There, with the hire of a harp for one and the purchase of some drawing paper for the other and all the finery they could already command, they meant to be very economical, very elegant, and very secluded with the hope, on Miss Beaufort's side, of praise and celebrity from all who walked within the sound of her instrument, and on Miss Letitia's, of curiosity and rapture in all who came near her while she sketched and to both, the consolation of meaning to be the most stylish girls in the place.

The particular introduction of Mrs. Griffiths to Miss Diana Parker secured them immediately an acquaintance with the Trafalgar House family and with the Denhams and the Miss Beauforts were soon satisfied with "the circle in which they moved in Sanditon," to use a proper phrase, for everybody must now "move in a circle"—to the prevalence of which rotatory motion is perhaps to be attributed the giddiness and false steps of many. Lady Denham had other motives for calling on Mrs. Griffiths besides attention to the Parkers. In Miss Lambe, here was the very young lady, sickly and rich, whom she had been asking for and she made the acquaintance for Sir Edward's sake and the sake of her milch asses. How it might answer with regard to the baronet remained to be proved but, as to the animals, she soon found that all her calculations of profit would be vain. Mrs. Griffiths would not allow Miss Lambe to have the smallest symptom of a decline or any complaint which asses' milk could possibly relieve. Miss Lambe was "under the constant care of an experienced physician" and his prescriptions must be their rule. And except in favor of some tonic pills, which a cousin of her own had a property in, Mrs. Griffiths never deviated from the strict medicinal page.

The corner house of the Terrace was the one in which Miss Diana Parker had the pleasure of settling her new friends and, considering that it commanded in front the favorite lounge of all the visitors at Sanditon and on one side whatever might be going on at the hotel, there could not have been a more favourable spot for the seclusion of the Miss Beauforts. And accordingly, long before they had suited themselves with an instrument or with drawing paper, they had, by the frequency of their appearance at the low windows upstairs in order to close the blinds, or open the blinds, to arrange a flowerpot on the balcony, or look at nothing through a telescope, attracted many an eye upwards and made many a gazer gaze again. A little novelty has a great effect in so small a place. The Miss Beauforts, who would have been nothing at Brighton, could not move here without notice. And even Mr. Arthur Parker, though little disposed for supernumerary exertion, always quitted the Terrace in his way to his brother's by this corner house for the sake of a glimpse of the Miss Beauforts, though it was half a quarter of a mile round about and added two steps to the ascent of the hill.

CHAPTER 11

Charlotte had been ten days at Sanditon without seeing Sanditon House, every attempt at calling on Lady Denham having been defeated by meeting with her beforehand. But now it was to be more resolutely undertaken, at a more early hour, that nothing might be neglected of attention to Lady Denham or amusement to Charlotte.

"And if you should find a favorable opening, my love," said Mr. Parker, who did not mean to go with them, "I think you had better mention the poor Mullins's situation and sound Her Ladyship as to a subscription for them. I am not fond of charitable subscriptions in a place of this kind, it is a sort of tax upon all that come. Yet as their distress is very great and I almost promised the poor woman yesterday to get something done for her, I believe we must set a subscription on foot, and, therefore, the sooner the better, and Lady Denham's name at the head of the list will be a very necessary beginning. You will not dislike speaking to her about it, Mary?"

"I will do whatever you wish me," replied his wife, "but you would do it so much better yourself. I shall not know what to say."

"My dear Mary," he cried. "It is impossible you can be really at a loss. Nothing can be more simple. You have only to state the present afflicted situation of the family, their earnest application to me, and my being willing to promote a little subscription for their relief, provided it meet with her approbation."

"The easiest thing in the world," cried Miss Diana Parker, who happened to be calling on them at the moment. "All said and done in less time than you have been talking of it now. And while you are on the subject of subscriptions, Mary, I will thank you to mention a very melancholy case to Lady Denham, which has been represented to me in the most affecting terms. There is a poor woman in Worcestershire, whom some friends of mine are exceedingly interested about, and I have undertaken to collect whatever I can for her. If you would mention the circumstance to Lady Denham! Lady Denham can give, if she is properly attacked. And I look upon her to be the sort of person who, when once she is prevailed on to undraw her purse, would as readily give ten guineas as five. And therefore, if you find her in a giving mood, you might as well speak in favor of another charity which I and a few more have very much at heart, the establishment of a Charitable Repository at Burton on Trent. And then there is the family of the poor man who was hung last assizes at York, though we really have raised the sum we wanted for putting them all out, yet if you can get a guinea from her on their behalf, it may as well be done."

"My dear Diana!" exclaimed Mrs. Parker, "I could no more mention these things to Lady Denham than I could fly."

"Where's the difficulty? I wish I could go with you myself. But in five minutes I must be at Mrs. Griffiths's to encourage Miss Lambe in taking her first dip. She is so frightened, poor thing, that I promised to come and keep up her spirits and go in the machine with her if she wished it. And as soon as that is over, I must hurry home, for Susan is to have leeches at one o' clock which will be a three hours' business. Therefore, I really have not a moment to spare. Besides that, between ourselves, I ought to be in bed myself at this present time for I am hardly able to stand, and when the leeches have done, I daresay we shall both go to our rooms for the rest of the day."

"I am sorry to hear it, indeed. But if this is the case I hope Arthur will come to us."

"If Arthur takes my advice, he will go to bed too, for if he stays up by himself he will certainly eat and drink more than he ought. But you see, Mary, how impossible it is for me to go with you to Lady Denham's."

"Upon second thoughts Mary," said her husband. "I will not trouble you to speak about the Mullinses. I will take an opportunity of seeing Lady Denham myself. I know how little it suits you to be pressing matters upon a mind at all unwilling." His application thus withdrawn, his sister could say no more in support of hers, which was his object, as he felt all their impropriety and all the certainty of their ill effect upon his own better claim. Mrs. Parker was delighted at this release and set off very happy with her friend and her little girl on this walk to Sanditon House.

It was a close, misty morning and, when they reached the brow of the hill, they could not for some time make out what sort of carriage it was which they saw coming up. It appeared at different moments to be everything from a gig to a phaeton, from one horse to four and, just as they were concluding in favor of a tandem, little Mary's young eyes distinguished the coachman and she eagerly called out, "It is Uncle Sidney, Mama, it is indeed." And so it proved. Mr. Sidney Parker, driving his servant in a very neat carriage, was soon opposite to them, and they all stopped for a few minutes.

The manners of the Parkers were always pleasant among themselves; and it was a very friendly meeting between Sidney and his sister-in-law, who was most kindly taking it for granted that he was on his way to Trafalgar House. This he declined, however. He was "just come from Eastbourne proposing to spend two or three days, as it might happen, at Sanditon" but the hotel must be his quarters. He was expecting to be joined there by a friend or two. The rest was common inquiries and remarks, with kind notice of little Mary, and a very well-bred bow and proper address to Miss Heywood, on her being named to him. And they parted to meet again within a few hours. Sidney Parker was about seven or eight and twenty, very good-looking, with a decided air of ease and fashion and a lively countenance. This adventure afforded agreeable discussion for some time. Mrs. Parker entered into all her husband's joy on the occasion and exulted in the credit that Sidney's arrival would give to the place.

The road to Sanditon House was a broad, handsome, planted approach between fields, leading at the end of a quarter of a mile through second gates into grounds which, though not extensive, had all the beauty and respectability which an abundance of very fine timber could give. These entrance gates were so much in a corner of the grounds or paddock, so near to one of its boundaries, that an outside fence was at first almost pressing on the road, till an angle here and a curve there threw them to a better distance. The fence was a proper park paling in excellent condition, with clusters of fine elms or rows of old thorns following its line almost everywhere. "Almost" must be stipulated, for there were vacant spaces, and through one of these, Charlotte, as soon as they entered the enclosure, caught a glimpse over the pales of something white and womanish in the field on the other side. It was something which immediately brought Miss Brereton into her head and, stepping to the pales, she saw indeed, and very decidedly in spite of the mist, Miss Brereton seated not far before her at the foot of the bank which sloped down from the outside of the paling and which a narrow path seemed to skirt along. Miss Brereton seated, apparently very composedly, and Sir Edward Denham by her side. They were sitting so near each other and appeared so closely engaged in gentle conversation that Charlotte instantly felt she had nothing to do but to step back again and say not a word. Privacy was certainly their object. It could not but strike her rather unfavorably with regard to Clara but hers was a situation which must not be judged with severity.

She was glad to perceive that nothing had been discerned by Mrs. Parker. If Charlotte had not been considerably the taller of the two, Miss Brereton's white ribbons might not have fallen within the ken of her more observant eyes. Among other points of moralizing reflection which the sight of this tête-à-tête produced, Charlotte could not but think of the extreme difficulty which secret lovers must have in finding a proper spot for their stolen interviews. Here perhaps they had thought themselves so perfectly secure from observation, the whole field open before them, a steep bank and pales never crossed by the foot of man at their back, and a great thickness of air to aid them as well! Yet here she had seen them. They were really ill-used.

The house was large and handsome. Two servants appeared to admit them and everything had a suitable air of property and order, Lady Denham valued herself upon her liberal establishment and had great enjoyment in the order and importance of her style of living. They were shown into the usual sitting room, well proportioned and well furnished, though it was furniture rather originally good and extremely well kept than new or showy. And as Lady Denham was not there, Charlotte had leisure to look about her and to be told by Mrs. Parker that the whole-length portrait of a stately gentleman which, placed over the mantelpiece, caught the eye immediately, was the picture of Sir Henry Denham and that one among many miniatures in another part of the room, little conspicuous, represented Mr. Hollis. Poor Mr. Hollis! It was impossible not to feel him hardly used. To be obliged to stand back in his own house and see the best place by the fire constantly occupied by Sir Henry Denham.

Too much concern over the fate of Mr. Hollis's spirit, despite his place in death having become secondary to his position in life, would detract focus from those creatures alive and vibrant and all amassed at Sanditon. Charlotte put aside thoughts of Lady Denham's husbands now she was in the lady's house, and, attempting to reform her opinions of the woman, she said aloud, "Poor Mr. Hollis, in such a crowd!" She was determined to think well of Lady Denham, however, but more due to force of will, and as a nod in the direction of etiquette, than any true inclination to view the woman as anything less than someone small in spirit but noticeably large of purse.

Mrs. Parker, who had not Charlotte's shrewd eye for analysis, relished the advantages that having the well-appointed sitting room unattended afforded her. She held no feelings of contempt for Lady Denham, on the contrary, her estimations led her to think the woman's character entirely in keeping with her situation, but she noted that success in absorbing all the details her inquisitive nature craved was best achieved in the lady's absence. Her eye was cast around; there were all those aspects that any woman familiar with the operations of housekeeping might pick out without meaning to do so with a view to criticism. The mantelpiece: was it free enough of dust to prove daily attentions? The floral display: was it fresh with upright blooms, rigid stems, and perky foliage as would speak of today's pickings? Mrs. Parker's expectations were entirely satisfied, all matters of homely comfort blended perfectly with the subtlest indications of grandeur.

The ambience at Sanditon House was the result of a rigorous housekeeping regimen and a good fortune. The sun had not been permitted to ravage this room. Some of the windows were bricked in and the blinds were more often down than up and the pristine condition of the furnishings, the well-rubbed mahogany and the paintings, proved such attention was worthwhile. The carpet was a new one, from Moorfields, London, with large octagons of crimson and gold. The plasterwork ceiling, should one's head be inclined upward, provided a pleasurable distraction; beasts entwined with fulsome fruits, insects, and ribands. This was by no means Mrs. Parker's first visit to Lady Denham's home, but the opportunity for unsupervised inspection was a novelty and her curiosity was satisfied in just one half of an hour. With Lady Denham away Mrs. Parker naturally took the lead in the proceedings, appearing at once knowledgeable and at ease with the place. Charlotte obliged her companion by playing the role of newcomer with such obliging and wide-eyed fascination as might win her acclaim in the theater.

"Is it not all you would expect, Charlotte my dear?" said Mrs. Parker. "The very picture of a home of significance?"

The younger turned to her elder, mindful to check her inclination to appear unimpressed. "Yes, it is very much as I expected, most significant," said she.

"Lady Denham has exactly the right number of servants you know, neither too little a band to be unequal to the demands of such a house, nor so large a throng as might cause inconvenience." Seeing Charlotte's expression, and judging her querulous, Mrs. Parker explained, "An excess of servants makes for as miserable a situation as having none at all. Too many mouths to feed, too many varying opinions as to result in discord and the increased possibility of a hapless chambermaid running off with an under-gardener." In a hushed tone she made further efforts to support her argument, confessing, "This sort of thing *has* happened, my dear Miss Heywood, it was the very fashion for some years. I think every great house must have suffered from the complaint at one time or another," then in an even lower whisper she went on, "I heard a tale, not so long ago enough as to render it less disquieting, of a butler, yes a *butler*—and quite a respected fellow at that—who went out of his wits for a parlormaid. The pair, disloyal scoundrels they proved themselves to be, dispatched, it is said, for Gretna without so much as a mention! The worst of it was that a whole ham and a soup ladle were discovered to have been misappropriated the following day. I ask you! A soup ladle! A ham! A whole one."

Charlotte heard this with a smile in her heart but a solemn countenance. "I wonder at the reasons for their choice."

Mrs. Parker was lively. "The reason, and here I am reliant on supposition only, was that they thought themselves in some sort of love, my dear! The restless often yearn to quit their sphere; a maid, depend upon it, would consider herself quite high in attaching to a butler. And it can puff an older man out of all sense of himself to have a young admirer languishing at his elbow." Here she paused to cast her eye quickly to her little girl who was apparently enthralled—if only such simple contentment could be achieved at home—by the intricacies of the carpet on which she sat. Persuaded that her daughter would be protected from the disreputable details she was about to disclose, Mrs. Parker, her voice still sunk to a mere whisper, confided, "I am more inclined to attribute their behavior to what I call animal cravings. Ungodly heathens!"

Charlotte laughed aloud before she could find the self-control to check herself. "Mrs. Parker," cried she, "I was referring to their taking a ham, a whole one, and a soup ladle. The two bear no relation and I can only think, though I am no specialist where mysteries are concerned, that the first they intended to eat and the second they proposed to sell."

Mrs. Parker shook her head but remained quiet. She was that breed of woman whose characteristics were somewhat quelled in her husband's presence. This morning, however, having been afforded the opportunity to voice her opinions quite without restraint, had given Charlotte more insight into the woman's personality than all her days in Sanditon had yet done. Mrs. Parker seemed to form her views quite without preconception and Charlotte suspected that she had no very firm belief in them. The sheer pleasure of being able to expound at will on this matter or another without too much interruption was obviously valued. Mrs. Parker was not at all harsh, her discourse erred more on the side of all that was jovial, even her most disparaging comments were made with the sort of half smile an avid gossiper wears.

Charlotte, who had liked Mrs. Parker a great deal prior to this morning, suddenly liked her all the more. She would not admit to being a great lover of gossip herself, but humorous conversation, especially that which consisted of scandals, was, as the human condition must dictate, relished. It did not escape Mrs. Parker's notice that the nature of her relationship with Miss Heywood had altered; there was now an easy companionship between the two. The elder felt assured that her young friend had not mistaken her for a bitter busybody and the younger was relieved to find these hitherto unknown facets of her companion's character.

The butler and the maid were not forgot, nor the ham in all its wholeness, nor the ladle. Charlotte, less eager to know the facts and more disposed to encourage her acquaintance's tendency to gossip, was compelled to inquire further. "The vulgar butler and the maid, which great house was it they disgraced? I should dearly love to know. There would be the something diverting in passing by there, as if perhaps admiring the grounds. I daresay I would smile to myself at such a house and its embarrassing history. Is the place within walking distance of Trafalgar House?"

Mrs. Parker threw up her hands. "Charlotte, my dear!" she said. "The setting for this bawdiest of tales was *not* Sanditon. *Our Sanditon*? Oh no, I must assure you, we have had no such disgraces sully this dear little town. Never has there been, to my knowledge at least, even a hint of scandal at Sanditon. Everything is eased here, all physical ills alleviated and even mental evils purified. You need look no farther than my own husband for all the information in the world. He is an expert on Sanditon."

"Indeed, he seems to be," said Charlotte, "he gives all and everything and more about his beloved resort with a passionate authority. I shall not falter then, if ever I wish to know all there can be to know about Sanditon's merits, I shall ask Mr. Parker without hesitation. I confess, though, that my mind is such that I seek proof too often. Could Mr. Parker give me some example of a truly wicked fellow made truly good by Sanditon I should build my faith on that, rather than hearsay."

"You have a curiously exacting nature for a woman," said Mrs. Parker, "and in one so young it is rare. Not that I think it to be entirely bad, but you may find such a propensity, which I usually judge to be the preserve of older, scholarly, men, will hinder any hopes of success in a romantic situation."

Charlotte laughed. "When it comes to the matter of a romantic situation I shall either be forced to tame my inclinations or I shall be obliged to attach to a person of like-mind. By your estimations, Mrs. Parker, I had best seek success with an ancient professor, besides, it will do me no harm to be as I am while at leisure, I am not actively seeking a husband."

"Then be sure of it, my dear," said the lady, "you will land one as soon as look at one and those avid seekers of fortune and fulfillment who go wildly out of their ways at the mere mention of an eligible gentleman will be left to gaze on in wonder."

"By your calculation I will have little control over the matter, I shall find a husband whether I desire one or not! Oh dear, the Miss Beauforts are destined to dislike me."

"This business of finding husbands is not to be viewed so lightly, Charlotte, there is something of an art to it you know, some consider it a talent; there are so many things to consider in the world of courtship. One must not make the wrong impression."

"Do not worry, my dear Mrs. Parker, I shall not run off with a butler."

Mrs. Parker sighed. "No, no, my dear, be sure you do not, there are to be no scandals at Sanditon, there never have been yet."

On leaving Sanditon House, for it was now clear that Lady Denham might not return for some time, the three began their walk back in the midmorning air. Mrs. Parker's attention was almost entirely taken up by her little girl's asking questions that began with "why." These inquiries were answered with a patient, "Well now, Alice" on each occasion with but a few exceptions. Soon the appeal of "why" had waned and "are" became the favorite of the child. She had not been so absorbed by the merits of the Moorfield carpet as her mother had supposed and demanded to know if all butlers were naughty and all chambermaids equally so. These issues could not be dealt with good-naturedly. Mrs. Parker, abashed at the effects her imprudence in talking of adult matters in the presence of a child had had, gave no response other than to hush her daughter as best she could by frowning at her.

The tantalizing white flash that had first caught Charlotte's attention was still there. Through the openings in the elms and thorns, Miss Brereton's ribbon was as visible to Charlotte as it had been on her first passing the place. Knowing that she might again be looking where she should not, she elected to avert her gaze, but found, on nearing the part that would give her the scene clearly, that she could not. Expecting (how rapidly intrigue grows) to find the lovers she found the area barren. The bank on which they had been sitting was now bereft of them.

But I saw Miss Brereton's ribbons, thought Charlotte. I am certain I saw them again, more convinced than when I first glimpsed them. She looked around her, the mist had cleared now and she grew evermore certain that she was not mistaken.

Mrs. Parker, with a very forlorn Alice at her side, walked at a steady pace ahead of Charlotte and she called out. "I must hurry along, my dear. With family in the neighborhood I expect a good deal of coming and going. If you will excuse me, I have no time for taking in the picturesque. I fear we have idled to excess at Sanditon House. Besides, thoughts of entertaining always blight my delight in the outdoors." Mrs. Parker's great relief now was that Lady Denham had not returned to the house during their visit. What chagrin would have resulted if Alice had spoken of eavesdropped tales of disgraced butlers and chambermaids in *her* presence. Another advantage to Lady Denham's absence was that Mrs. Parker had been relieved of any obligation to speak of either her husband's or her sister-in-law's good causes. To be saved the mortification of rallying for funds was a blessing; she would explain this failure to her husband and his sister later. The Worcestershire woman, the Charitable Repository in Burton on Trent, and the family of the hanged man might all be poorer for the fact as would be the Mullinses, but Mrs. Parker was, nevertheless, as happy as a person who has acknowledged her own folly can be.

There was relief to be had on Charlotte's part, too. Mrs. Parker's departure was most welcome. Charlotte waved to her, and to the now low-spirited little Alice, quelling what might have been deemed her unmannerly enthusiasm. She could now take in the scene that was the cause of her fascination. "I was not mistaken!" she exclaimed aloud. "That is not a flower or seagull's feather, it *is* Miss Brereton's ribbon, or something like it, and now I am all eagerness no know why the owner has discarded her adornment and left it hung like that on a bush." Charlotte assured herself that Mrs. Parker was out of sight, waiting a while lest the woman might find cause to turn on her heel to call out to her, then she slipped through a space in the elms and headed toward the empty bank. The white flash, clear and snowy in the bright sun, urged her to quicken her step and caused her curiosity to pique. The area of grass, where Charlotte had not an hour before seen Clara Brereton sitting in an intimate posture with Edward Denham, was flattened down, noticeably so in contrast to the unified carpet that surrounded it. The ribbon, or what had at first appeared to be such, was there just as she thought, strung on a thorn on a bush. But it appeared snagged there by accident, not contrived to hang. Charlotte knew immediately that it was not the trimming she had first supposed. The silky remnant was a tattered piece of a garment. Part of a sleeve? On closer inspection it appeared to be a collar. Indeed it was a collar! "Clara Brereton does not seem such a girl, and these kinds of things, I am told, *do not* happen at Sanditon. Why then, would a seemingly respectable young woman see fit to remove her collar when unchaperoned in the company of a man?" said Charlotte to herself. "Even my sensibilities are rocked, and I think I might judge myself to be as liberal-minded as can be acceptable!"

The necessity to remove the collar from the bush became immediate. Its visibility to passersby, even those distant from the scene, was known to Charlotte. The pure whiteness that had attracted her attention could just as easily attract another's. This must be avoided. Nervousness was upon her although she was not prone to it and she tore the collar swiftly from its wrongful place. Now, to get away. If Clara should return in pursuit of the lost lace Charlotte should feel embarrassed, worse than that, Sir Edward Denham might stroll down the bank and find her there. Hesitation took hold and for a while she simply stood there with the collar creased in her hand.

The first small cry she did not startle to, so shaken by her own imprudence was she, but the second clearer moan she could not dismiss. The direction of the whimper she could not have determined but the rustling of leaves took her to a small clearing where she found its source. Miss Clara Brereton, her face as pale as her sprigged muslin, was there disposed. Half sitting, half flung, it seemed, into state of indignity and discomfiture all at once. Charlotte could not contain her horror and knew that an unladylike expression had escaped her lips before she could control herself. On seeing Charlotte the young Miss Brereton began to cry, relieved at being discovered and terrified that she would not be fit to conceive a credible, if false, explanation for her demise. Her hair was all about her face and her expression was one of mortification.

"Clara, stay calm and I shall get help," said Charlotte.

The girl was quick to protest. "No, Miss Heywood, *please*, I shall be recovered quite soon, if you could help me up."

Reluctant to move the injured girl Charlotte pleaded that more damage could be caused by moving her before seeking proper advice. Miss Brereton's defense in this matter could not be disallowed.

"We have no doctor at Sanditon, Miss Heywood, so your opinion would be as good as any."

The girl spoke the truth. Of course there was no doctor at Sanditon, had there been such she would never have been there. For Mr. Parker would never have ventured to Willingden on the strength of his misreading a newspaper article and he should never have sprained his ankle. In not enduring such an injury he would have been deprived of being introduced into her home for the means of recovery and would therefore never had had the opportunity to encourage her thither to Sanditon. Such are the convolutions of life.

"Ah, Sanditon," said Charlotte with some frustration, "is *all* that is restorative and good!"

Miss Brereton, with Charlotte's assistance, was jostled upright, the latter suspecting that the former made far less of her injuries than she might. Out on the more open ground Charlotte and Clara sat, fatigued by exertion and wounds respectively.

"I daresay I should explain the mishap that led to my falling over," said Miss Brereton, quietly. This Charlotte was eager to hear, her suspicions about the case had already risen to such heights as to condemn Sir Edward Denham as a vicious seducer and she was keen to learn how the apparently guileless Clara would contrive to invent an explanation for her demise. While the girl seemed taken up with concocting a story, Charlotte slipped the collar into the revers of her own sleeve.

"I often walk this bank alone," began Clara, "I enjoy it in the mornings, it is known I walk here … alone."

"I have no reason to doubt it, Miss Brereton, but your status, whether alone or accompanied, is of little consequence, I think it more important to know how you came to … stumble."

"Oh yes," said Clara, uneasy, "there was an uneven part to the ground that I had not noticed before, a ridge or a raised part, I cannot say, my foot was caught on a bramble or a branch, a root, it might have been a root, and without warning I had fallen, quite to the ground."

The collar, now creasing in its hiding place in Charlotte's sleeve, was sure to be missed from the girl's neck when she returned to the house. Charlotte's preference was to ignore the matter entirely but, whatever unpleasantness had befallen Clara, she was convinced that the girl would not want to arouse Lady Denham's suspicions by returning home in such a peculiar state of undress. Having witnessed the attention to detail in that lady's home not an hour before, she was persuaded that all particulars concerning anyone connected to her. would be observed. Clara then must be in danger, at the very least, of the severest of reprimands. Had she not realized, due to her discomposure, that she was so exposed?

"Do you usually elect to walk without a collar, Clara?" The instinctive movement of the girl's hand to her neck, her quick glance to her bosom, and her suddenly drawn breath all foretold of the expected. Although Charlotte had long known the girl's loss, the young woman herself was only first discovering it.

"Oh!" exclaimed she, "where can it ... " She broke off, words would reveal nothing, her expression revealed all. Charlotte, without explanation, jumped up and headed back in the direction of the bush on which she had first found Miss Brereton's collar.

"Clara," she said with a feigned look of inspiration, "I have just recalled something that I earlier overlooked, I think I know just the place you mislaid your collar and if you can wait a moment for me I shall go to get it for you."

Miss Brereton's surprise was apparent. "But how, and, oh … but where do you think I mislaid it?"

"Just a little way along the bank, I distinctly remember a glimpse of white, your collar is, of course, white, Miss Brereton, is it not?"

"Oh yes, yes it is."

"Then let me get it for you, for it will not do to head home without it."

"But I shall walk with you, Miss Heywood, it is not so far to that part of the bank, I daresay I shall be able to conceal any tears in the lace, if there are any, of course. And if it is not too far to go."

"Of course," said Charlotte helping the girl to her feet. She was now taken up entirely by the devising of a plan, how to take the collar from her own cuff and give the appearance of happening upon it on the grass. It was not Charlotte's usual style to resort to devious measures, she despised deceitful behavior in others and abhorred it in herself but could see no other way to assist and protect the unfortunate girl. Their advance to the little area of the bank in question was slow; when they were within a few yards of it, Charlotte quickened her pace, and then she ran.

"I can see it," she called, "Miss Brereton, your collar, I can see it!" She made a show of dashing ahead, took on the actions of one stooping to pick something up and with her back turned to Miss Brereton and her left side partly hidden by bushes, pulled the collar from its place of concealment. Waving it frantically, she called out, "Is this it, Miss Brereton?" Before Clara could answer Sir Edward Denham was behind Charlotte, she started violently when he spoke.

"Good Heavens, Miss Heywood," said he. "What in the name of goodness do you think you are doing brandishing Miss Brereton's garments about the place?" Then, as if his voice had not caused alarm enough, he hooked his arm about hers and proceeded, with an alarmingly firm grasp, to march her in the general direction of Sanditon House. Miss Brereton did not earn his acknowledgment. What a peculiar person he was, on the one hand full of poetry and sentiment, on the other callus and insupportably selfish. These were the manners of a true seducer. Powerful manners. But poor Miss Brereton! In the morning she had been fixed in his gaze, no doubt aroused by his preposterous, but effective, method of poetic allurement. The very next she had been subjected to Heaven knew what, resulting in the sorry state that now defined her. Yet he, so definitely the offender, was not inclined to show her the slightest concern. It was too much for Charlotte.

"I think you might employ your time better by offering your arm and your firm support to Miss Brereton," she urged. "She has been the victim of an incident this morning and I judge she is weakened by the experience."

Sir Edward Denham smiled. "Miss Brereton," he said with an emphasis that could not be ignored but would certainly be overheard, "should not put herself into the kinds of positions that encourage incidents to occur. I have no sympathy for her."

"That is quite apparent, Sir," said Charlotte, "but if you will not offer her your support then I am afraid I must take leave of you and offer her mine." Charlotte released herself from his possession and turned to find Miss Brereton making slow but steady progress toward her. "Your collar, Clara," said Charlotte proffering the garment to its owner. "Put it on, it is a little puckered but it will serve well enough until you can replace it with another."

Miss Brereton set about wrapping and tucking the sad looking scrap about her person. Sir Edward Denham waited, with an air of impatience, just a short way ahead of them. Charlotte wished he had walked ahead, she could not bear the embarrassment she felt for Miss Brereton nor the disgust she felt for Sir Edward Denham. Oh, he who had certain expectations to live up to seemed equal to none of them. He was good-looking to be sure but possession of good looks in a man of a lascivious demeanor make him all the more dangerous. Charlotte, mortified that she could so readily have approved of him once, was determined that she could not any longer like him. What was an intelligent man of fair fortune and good breeding doing going about the world with the express purpose of seduction? Why had not Sanditon's purifying air had the effect of driving out his evils? He had surely breathed enough of it in—his lengthy style of discourse, his penchant for extensive verbalizing, and his love of a prefix or ten, would have dictated that he had done so. Such a person, such an avid speaker, has his mouth open far more often than others do.

As the two ladies neared, Sir Edward Denham made clear that his inclination was to favor Miss Heywood, again her arm was forcibly linked with his, and the situation, the atmosphere, and the conversation were all uneasy. He was unlike any person Charlotte had ever occasioned to meet in her life. She hoped he was unique. To meet more than one such person in a lifetime would be misfortune indeed. Neither her sharp mind nor her sense of fairness would allow her to be influenced by his elegant appearance or accomplished manners. He was, throughout his very being, the epitome of dishonesty and selfishness. Miss Brereton did not utter a word during their walk back to Sanditon House, the responses to Sir Edward's comments all had to be Charlotte's, the difficulty being that what she felt strongly compelled to say was left unsaid and what she actually said meant nothing and in no way reflected her actual feelings.

Returned to the house, Charlotte thought with irony on the very different natures of her two visits to the place that day. Lady Denham was now at home and the sitting room, despite the portraits of her deceased husbands, was entirely filled with her presence. She did not seem in as amiable mood as befitted a rich woman on a sunny day and Charlotte wondered if the news of Miss Brereton's incident would prove to distract her from her misery or further plunge her into it. Sir Edward greeted Lady Denham with a kiss on each cheek, but it seemed without genuine feeling. The lady received Charlotte graciously, gesturing for her to take up a seat nearby. "You find me quite fatigued, Miss Heywood, I have been about the place this morning, the mists are quite my remedy you know and I always take the trouble of inhalation whenever I can. My fatigue is not to concern you. It is merely a side effect of my moisture intake. Some people cannot take the moisture, themselves being somewhat sodden to start with, but I always feel the benefit of inner lubrication."

Charlotte could do nothing but agree whilst noting to herself that the residents of Sanditon were amongst the oddest creatures imaginable. Sir Edward Denham paced the room and at that moment, Clara, who had been taken up with replacing her collar, returned looking remarkably refreshed.

Teas were on the table, and a selection of sandwiches, which Lady Denham ignored. "Ah, Clara my dear!" she cried, "your walk this morning was beneficial?"

There was no more than a "Yes, ma'am," as a response.

Charlotte was bemused. Sir Edward was quick to interject; the edge to his voice did not go unnoticed by Charlotte. "Miss Brereton lost her collar by the bank, apparently."

"Oh, not the white-work piece?" cried Lady Denham. " I shall be mortified if it were that one, you know it is such a perfect example."

"Madam, do not be alarmed, the collar is found, but in need of a little repair, I came across it myself while walking the area," said Charlotte.

"Clara walks the area with regularity," said Sir Edward to Charlotte and when it became clear that he had nothing more to say on the matter Lady Denham felt herself obliged to add but one firmly spoken word.

"Alone," said she.

In that instant, Charlotte felt the whole group conspiring to mislead her. Miss Brereton was sitting with a contented air about her, no signs of her previous distress were immediately discernable, and she made no effort to explain to Lady Denham that she had been involved in an incident. Sir Edward did not offer up the subject although this fact was not so startling to Charlotte for she believed his silence on the matter to be the result of his wishing to conceal some unpleasant truth. Lady Denham was disinclined to talk after taking the mists, stating that talking allowed some of the restorative vapors to escape from the inner body therefore rendering the entire process of inhalation pointless. With the lady of the house inclined to silence, the others were obliged to remain quiet and the party eventually dispersed with Sir Edward Denham announcing that he was to call on the Miss Beauforts, Clara Brereton electing to visit the library, and Charlotte heading gratefully toward Trafalgar House with such feelings of astonishment as she had never owned before.

CHAPTER 12

When Mrs. Parker was over her dismay at Charlotte's lengthy absence, she set about the task of informing her that Mr. Parker had an appointment to call on the Miss Beauforts and that he would be heartily glad of her return, as his wish was that she should accompany him. She had reprimanded poor little Alice for eavesdropping and told her husband that Lady Denham could not be prevailed upon to support either the Mullinses' or his sister's stream of causes due to having been absent during their visit. On the subject of his intention to formally introduce himself to the Miss Beauforts, she was nothing but animated.

"My dear Miss Heywood, my husband would feel so much more at ease if you were to accompany him, to take the lead in feminine conversation. Mr. Parker is fully aware that his conversation might be too much of Sanditon and business matters for the young ladies. Your presence will alleviate this."

Charlotte's wish was to remain at Trafalgar House, she had heard little of the Miss Beauforts that encouraged her to want to be acquainted with them but, due to a feeling of being bound to do so, she consented to the visit. She was, in all honesty, urged, prompted, and nudged into agreeing. Visits were everything in Sanditon, the encouragement of newcomers was a religion, a necessity, a matter of life or debts. For newcomers bring new wealth, which, if they are favorably received, they are inclined to spread about the place. Old or new, money could never be ignored. And so it was that Charlotte Heywood found herself setting off as friend to Mr. Parker to call on the Miss Beauforts. The very idea of them wearied her. Fashionable young ladies, those who are fashionable to a very particular degree, were generally conceited and

Charlotte had not the energy to enthuse about the prospect of spending time with their like. She was likely, she mused, to be thought too much a country girl to be accepted by them.

The much-spoken-of Miss Beauforts were exactly as Charlotte had expected. Prettyish girls, splendidly dressed, whose splendor seemed too much the result of misconceived ideas of elegance. Their ribbons were too brightly colored, their corsets too obviously boosting, and their manner of fluttering their fans by their faces altogether too contrived to be accepted as a natural inclination. Even in the privacy of their sitting room, the Miss Beauforts seemed to feel themselves on parade. And the setting, which had the fashionable look of industry about it, was perfection itself. There was music at the spinnet, a writing case (open) at a small round pedestal table, a work box and books stacked, opened, and scattered about the place, even the sofa was drawn up nearer to the table. A harp—every one of its forty-one strings would later be discussed and admired—and artist's tools and achievements completed the picture. This was to be something of an exhibition and the Miss Beauforts displayed themselves with every belief that they represented the finest examples of beauty. In their own way they had about them an air of elegance, their complexions were good as was to be expected, and hoped for, in girls so young, though Charlotte detected traces of rouge. Their voices were cultured, and they were, without doubt, accomplished. They had no compunction in recommending themselves to new acquaintances.

Their particular appeal, however, was ever increased by there being *two* Miss Beauforts. Here was, in Charlotte's experience, a very definite case to be argued. *Two* sisters, even if plain, seemed to have about them a mystical allure that young men or otherwise could not resist. Three or more sisters would merely confuse a gentleman, and one girl with no sisters or rivals lacked all of those charms. Charlotte concluded with conviction that the Miss Beauforts exemplified this rule and she felt sure they had used it to their advantage in the past and were very likely to depend upon it in the future.

The musical Miss Beaufort, who had a sharper nose and more determined look than her sister, was eager to exhibit her talents to her new acquaintances and she struck up on her harp. The artistic Miss Beaufort displayed some of her drawings to the room. She was not without an eye for symmetry or form and her pieces were excellent in quality. It occurred to Charlotte that these sisters, these two girls so prone to flaunt their attributes, had mastered the art of a virtually symbiotic existence where neither girl's magnetism would detract from the merits of the other. Their chosen pastimes were so intrinsically compatible as to ensure equal attention was always bestowed on both girls. The musical sister would play while the artistic sister drew or showed off her masterpieces. Admirers could *listen* and *look*, all at once. Their unity and their affinity were thus displayed that afternoon with the one girl's pleasant strains on the harp being every bit the accompaniment that the other's gallery of sketches demanded. Simultaneous admiration was thence awarded and the Miss Beauforts, bright, sparkling, narcissistic creatures that they were, bathed in it.

Mr. Parker, although happily married, had not lost his liking for pretty females and relished being the only man in their audience. Charlotte felt herself very plain and provincial while in the orbit of the sophisticated Miss Beauforts. And French names indeed, thought she, the height of fashion! That was the very impression to give at a small gathering in a small, English seaside town. Quite ladies of the world they promoted themselves as. They were templates; beings torn from La Belle Assemblée; with their pained talk of not yet having decided on the benefits of veils when parasols were surely considered prettier.

All members of the party took some coffee and some cakes, with the exception of the Miss Beauforts who drank the coffee but declined the Maids of Honor with looks of abhorrence and very strong representations about the risks to their figures and their complexions. They each consented to a small piece of bread; though economy of appetite appeared to be the only restriction they imposed upon themselves. In all else, they were extravagant.

When refreshments had all been had, Mr. Parker and Charlotte, who had each decided that the introduction could now be considered fully established, were about to take their leave when another addition to the party was made which, by necessity, increased the length of their stay.

Of Miss Lambe, they had had intelligence, but the information had been too scant to entirely forewarn them of her exact character. She was known to be substantially wealthy and seen, upon her arrival, to be abominably thin and considered too precious, too sweet, and too delicate for her own good. Where creed and color had mixed, Miss Lambe had skin the hue of which put Charlotte in mind of the creamy coffee the party had just enjoyed; her eyes, so dark and languid, were contrastingly shiny in her dusky and pretty face. Miss Lambe had undoubtedly earned the honor of being Mrs. Griffiths's favorite charge and the latter ushered the girl forth into the sitting room with an attitude of panicky reverence; ensuring *hers* was the most comfortable chair and taking care to check that the draft from the window would not have ill effect. Where Charlotte had noticeably paled in the company of the glittering Miss Beauforts, they now knew their own charms to be diluted. Miss Lambe's beauty was of the serious kind that needs no adornment. Her simple muslin dress was of the best quality, expertly sewn and exquisitely tailored to her delicate frame. She wore an understated topaz crucifix and no other embellishments. She did not speak, it seemed to Charlotte that her only concession to the procedure of being introduced to those she did not know was to smile and incline her head very carefully as if overdoing the gesture could actually break her neck. It soon became clear that Mrs. Griffiths's delight was to talk on behalf of her young charge and it was through the exuberant woman that the party learned about Miss Lambe's first excursion into the sea.

"Goodness me, what a remedy! Your dear sister," this to Mr. Parker, "elected to go into the machine with poor Miss Lambe. What a kind soul Diana Parker is. The waves were quite at a peak today, I think they quite alarmed Miss Lambe. Did they not, dear?"

This last was emphasized with a quick look at her charge but thereafter Mrs. Griffiths's attention, once more, was devoted to Mr. Parker, who, on hearing such praise of his sister and his Sanditon and indeed his waves, thought it very fortunate that he had not left early. He was all delight.

Mrs. Griffiths continued, "Your good sister had not a shred of hesitation about the matter, the waves, she assured us, would only serve to agitate the remedial deposits of the seabed, so indeed it was fortuitous because Miss Lambe's single immersion has had the effect of two or maybe three such treatments. She does look markedly improved in color, posture, and humor. The dippers, I daresay, felt the benefit of the lively sea, the horses, mind, were not in the mood. I have never been in a machine that rocked and rattled so. I am always comfortable in one though, I need the protection. I so dread coming across men bathing since the King has made it the trend to immerse *unclothed*."

"*I* was only ever in a bathing machine at Weymouth where I drank the water, not through choice I might add. It did me no good at all, the salt is harsher there, I daresay, than here," said Charlotte.

Mr. Parker could not disguise the delight he felt in spending time in such company. Mrs. Griffiths was so violently struck with Sanditon that he felt confident of persuading her to visit every year. She would, he was certain, bring with her a good number of sickly, but rich, young women. Sanditon dominated the conversation; all that Charlotte had heard before was repeated and other snippets, which she had *not* yet been party to, were revealed. She was sure to be subjected to more such details in the future. There was little chance of reminding Mr. Parker that their intention had been to leave at least thirty minutes before. He was engrossed. He was enraptured. They were afforded no break in his unstoppable stream of chatter. Miss Letitia Beaufort, fully aware that Miss Lambe was enjoying the attention she, Letitia, felt herself and her sister to deserve, strolled to the window. Her guise was that of cooling herself, of taking the air, but her intention was to throw a look to her sister without the others of the party being aware of it.

She was now heartily tired of Mr. Parker, his attentions had turned so dramatically from her sister and herself to Mrs. Griffiths and Miss Lambe and she wished him gone immediately. Standing there by the casement, her dejection soon dissipated upon seeing Sir Edward Denham, or who she suspected to be him, approaching their lodgings.

"More visitors, cherie," said she to her sister, affectedly. They had both adopted the fashionable habit of mingling French words with English.

"Who is it?"

"If I am not mistaken, it is Sir Edward Denham himself," said Letitia, still peeping from behind the drapes. "Yes! It can only be he; too finely dressed to be any other, I am convinced his green coat is taken from the wonderful pattern we admired in Le Beau Monde."

"And is he handsome?" inquired her sister.

"Soon you shall see."

Charlotte smiled to herself, was Sanditon truly the curative place it was purported to be? Its inhabitants all had about them a sort of healthful smugness, and suddenly the Miss Beauforts' complexions, demeanor, deportment, and enthusiasm were all inordinately improved, but that was caused by the mere mention of a man, no seabathing ever had so fast an effect. How shameful to be a woman, a member of such a sex, but how much worse to be a man and be the prey of such pretty vultures! Even Sir Edward Denham could not be a match for these two. His expertise in deceitful charm may have afforded him successful conquests in the past but this was sure to be a new situation. He was beaten before he had begun, before he had entered the room. Charlotte was certain of it. He was outnumbered; he would be overcome. The two Miss Beauforts could well prove too much, even for him.

The sisters were soon afforded the opportunity of appraising just how handsome a fellow Sir Edward Denham was. Soon after Letitia had announced his arrival, he was brought into the room. An expression of pleasure appeared on his face on his noticing

Charlotte but it soon departed and was swiftly replaced by another. He had his first glimpse of the sisters. Oh! Where to direct his eyes, which pretty face to gaze upon first and which to stare at longest! He observed the two young women, who he assumed to be the Miss Beauforts, sitting together on a chaise, each held a fan close up to their mouths so that only their hungry eyes were to be seen. On being introduced to them (Mr. Parker presented the young women as if they were princesses or duchesses at worst), Sir Edward bowed and the young women twittered, but it was impossible to ascertain which twitter came from which girl for the fans remained aloft, coquettishly positioned, and obscured their pretty mouths. Such fluttering was an aptitude, one only acquired with practice. They carried it off well.

"Oh, dismay is all mine," thought Charlotte. "Surely he is not so impressive as to render two adult girls to dissolve so!" Sir Edward Denham greeted her with courtesy, she responded likewise. "Good afternoon, Sir," said she.

He moved close in to her and bent to whisper. "*You* have not taken to giggling behind a fan then, Miss Heywood?" he breathed.

"No indeed, Sir, I have not," she retorted, "for in the first place I find nothing much to giggle about and in the second I do not have a fan."

Sir Edward Denham smiled and put his mouth to her ear again. "But of course, Miss Heywood," he purred, "you would not need a fan, for what in the world could cause a clearheaded girl like yourself to be in need of cooling off."

Charlotte knew very well his intention to be that of flustering her, embarrassing her. He was abominable! But she had to confess that the arts he so cleverly employed were not entirely lost on her. He had been so close to her! Good Heavens, the intimacy of whispering ought to be avoided in public whenever possible. The caress of his breath, he whom she hated so violently, still seemed to linger and she resented him for it. The idea that he seemed determined to pursue her was quickly gone, for he was soon in the process of being introduced to Miss Lambe and, Charlotte noted with amusement and relief, he now wore a very different expression on his face. He had about him that mercurial quality that allowed dramatic alteration to take place with rapidity. His bow to Miss Lambe was lower and longer than the gesture he had made to the tittering Miss Beauforts, but Miss Lambe's fortune often bought her a longer lower bow than her less fortunate friends.

"Miss Lambe, it is an honor," he gushed on making the girl's acquaintance. She rewarded him with no more than her customary smile and faint nod. This rendered her all the more intriguing to him. The Miss Beauforts could not sit too long observing him, this man who so fascinated them, in pursuit of another and Letitia once more ensured that attention was drawn to her and her sister by taking up her stool and beginning on the harp. During her previous performance, she had not mentioned having any particular difficulty turning pages or reading music, but now she pleaded, "I will play of course, but must have someone to turn pages for me." She looked about the room.

Sir Edward, with such an appearance of gallantry, was by her in an instant. He was the natural choice, the very person to oblige.

"You are too kind, Sir," said she sweetly and, seated in that ungainly way that is the posture of harpists, she went on, "but do draw up a low chair for yourself, for I fear the sheets are set too far down for a person of your great stature."

With his height and gallantry so flattered and admired, Sir Edward was in her grip. What an attitude of devotion this man so easily adopted and how readily the girl drank in his admiring glances. The other Miss Beaufort, mindful to have her share of the attention, began a turn about the room and chanced to drop her fan by Sir Edward's feet. The effect of the appeal of one sister did not overcome him so much that he could not pay proper attention to the other. Courtesy was not lost to him. His retrieving her ornament and placing it back in her grateful hand was less cleanly executed than it might have been, for Charlotte noticed that with the return of the girl's possession there came also the briefest brushing of fingers. Now the artistic Miss Beaufort, who had since been introduced as Davina, was more in need of her fan than ever. Her blushes and flustered countenance were noticed by all, and would very likely be regarded by Sir Edward Denham as a sure sign of his own charisma.

Could every female in the world be so taken by Sir Edward Denham? Was she, Charlotte, the only steady-minded young woman who would not be smitten? Where would his activities lead? What good could come of his addiction to flirtation? Moreover, how many more young girls would find themselves strewn in the hedgerows minus their collars? Sir Edward Denham seemed to her more a beast than a man; but a beautiful beast he made and all who saw him seemed to fall unavoidably in some sort of love, to be lured, bewitched, mesmerized by his charms. Apart from Charlotte, who knew herself opposed to loving such an animal unless there was a very strong chance of taming him, and that, she felt, was unlikely. Here was a creature certain to bite. Thus, although willing to admit that he had a certain appealing way about him, Charlotte determined always to think ill of him and vowed never allow him to whisper in her ear in a public place again.

Chapter 13

Some newcomers to a place have the art of fitting in immediately. Once a day or so has passed, these visitors give the impression of having always been part of that sphere. Residents accept them as familiar and welcome them as old friends. Not once did Charlotte think herself this sort of person. She was well received in Sanditon and liked, as far as she knew, but she had, and gave, the impression that she was not quite living life, there was always that quality that made her and those about her feel she was distanced, for the sake of observation, from central circumstances. Charlotte Heywood could sit in a room filled with people and not quite be there. Born and raised in a large and noisy family, this ability to detach herself and think herself elsewhere had been a useful facility in times past.

Sanditon was such a place; its residents so peculiar to her that she could not feel related to them and struggled to understand them. Their ideas, mostly irrational, prevented her from viewing a single one of them as entirely sound-minded and there was nothing that unsettled Charlotte more than a tendency toward absurdity. Wit, she had all the time in the world for. But it seemed that humor was sadly lacking in the Parker family, at least in those members of it she had met. Oh, they were amusing, comedic almost, but unwittingly so. Mr. Parker, dear sweet man that he was, could certainly not be described as conventional. Always talking about Sanditon in his impassioned manner, he expected every other human being to join in his craze and, worse still, he positively delighted in hearing about people's illnesses. Ill people were Mr. Parker's pleasure and were to be Sanditon's great salvation. They would flock there in time and the magical cures afforded them would be just the promotion the place and its staunchest advocate longed for. Mr. Parker liked nothing better than to hear news of a particularly bad cold that was circulating the world. It was his delight to imagine the sick, in their sniffling droves, heading toward his glorious little bit of Sussex with their full reticules and high fevers. The surest way to unsettle Mr. Parker was to mention Bath!

"Ah, that unclean hovel," he once proclaimed, "what possible remedy can be found in so built up an area? People have been driven quite out of their senses over the dreadful place but I cannot understand what the pump rooms have that my dear Sanditon does not. The waters, I grant you, may well be restorative, but what use is immersion or consumption in such a place as Bath? The smoke and confusion of it all would quickly render any medicinal intakes entirely useless! The percussion of the streets drives one distracted. The ground is so filthy everyone must wear pattens and the dreadful things are so noisy everyone must be obliged to suffer a headache as a result. No one ever thinks of pattens in Sanditon, we have such pristine footpaths. And headaches have a pleasing way of passing quickly. Spas, in general you know, are not so popular these days since the King got himself ill at Cheltenham."

Then there was Brinshore; he could never comprehend the success of that place. "Brighton, I grant you, is pleasant enough and the Prince of Wales's patronage has made it fashionable. There they have the advantage of the *ton*. Even the Kent coast, these last two years or so, has made something of a mark. Londoners, we must at least admire their fierceness of spirit, go by steamboat from the Thames to Margate, you know. I concede there might be benefits in the place, in Kent generally perhaps, but the return to London must surely undo any good." What, he wondered, could any of these places offer that his own beloved Sanditon did not? His entire existence revolved around Sanditon. He cherished it. He swanned in adoration through its streets, breathing its salty restorative air while his head filled with plans, theories, and concepts. Advancement and promotion were his objectives. Schemes and questions rallied for attention in his mind. How many more visitors could be encouraged? How could the place become more widely known?

His latest project, to install a professional, conventional medicine man was brought about, not by any belief on his part that such an authority was needed. Moreover, his calculations had led him to deduce that half the population of the world must be sound-minded enough to seek natural cures for their ills and the other half was made up of those committed to chemical assistance. To lure this latter half to Sanditon, he must have a doctor reside there. Even his own poor family's violent feelings about the failures of doctors might well be eased once such a man could be made known to them. Pills, potions, lotions, and unguents were not Mr. Parker's own favored remedies but if a substantial portion of potential visitors could be persuaded to head for his beloved part of the coast on the strength of such treatments being available, then he must not give up his quest to find a man qualified and trusted to prescribe such therapies.

Mrs. Parker bore her husband's exuberance with saintly tolerance. Quiet agreement was her favored stance. She had no very strong inclinations to contradict or question. Mr. Parker's energy was best flung in the direction of Sanditon. An entire neighborhood could far easier absorb his excitement than a single person ever could. Mrs. Parker was satisfied that he was not without direction; it suited her very well indeed. She had the house and the family; four children were quite enough to keep her occupied. It had occurred to her that had Mr. Parker's vigor not been reserved for Sanditon, she might have been obliged to mother an even larger brood, for she was fully sensible of the force of her husband's passions and believed that such energy must be spent somewhere. Mrs. Parker was rather grateful not to be the mother of a fine family of ten. She had seen many a poor animal worn down by motherhood.

The occupants of Sanditon, those who moved in Lady Denham's luxuriant sphere, were not people Charlotte Heywood had a natural inclination to like, but there was no denying they were enigmatic. Miss Brereton, poor beautiful Miss Brereton, with her frail appearance, seemed to Charlotte to have more fortitude than was at first apparent. Hers was a deceptive meekness. Her rapid recovery after the incident on the bank had left Charlotte intrigued and Sir Edward Denham's harsh treatment of the girl simply could not be explained or excused no matter how many times Charlotte dwelt on the subject. Lady Denham was, as many rich women before her have been, unaware of and unconcerned by the realities of the world, unless one could consider Sanditon "the world" and what went on within it "reality." Lady Denham inspired indifference in Charlotte, she was not so bad as to induce any feelings of strong dislike, nor so wholly good or appealing in manner to encourage admiration. But of all the residents, it was Sir Edward that Charlotte most adamantly despised. What could be liked about him? A girl of good sense, as Charlotte considered herself to be, would not be drawn in by his charming manners and looks. If she was drawn in at all, and she was loathe to admit it if she was, the allure would be nothing more than would be expected of her inquisitive nature. If she thought about him, it was never with soft reflection, when he came into her mind it was only because some aspect of his horrendous character puzzled her.

The newcomers fascinated Charlotte: the Miss Beauforts, Miss Lambe, and Mrs. Griffiths. The latter held the least fascination, there was nothing unexpected about her at all; she was merely the proud hen presiding over her small brightly colored chicks. The brightest, the Miss Beauforts, were certainly man-hunting, the sweetest, Miss Lambe, who was the most eligible of them all, was certainly not. Mr. Parker's sisters and brother Arthur, who Charlotte had already had occasion to observe, were all three hypochondriacs, though their psychosomatic complaints differed vastly. There was, however, in their existence, a harmonic tone despite their constant reprimands to each other over matters of health care.

Arthur, great butter-devouring, idle Arthur, was a polite young man but reason had long deserted him. He had lived too much in the company of fussing sisters and this had resulted in his manner being quite unlike that of other young men. Susan and Diana had molded soft Arthur, he was the malleable child neither of them had ever had, the bendable husband neither of them had ever wanted, and the very thing to worry themselves sick over that they craved. "Poor Arthur is quite sallow today!" "Poor Arthur's tongue is very pale." "Poor Arthur has been poisoned by green tea." Poor Arthur, indeed. He was prodded, examined, massaged, purged, leeched, and bled at the slightest sign of affliction.

Diana Parker, who proclaimed to be sicker than the rest of the family put together, showed little sign of being so. Always occupied with business other than her own, her pride was that she would help anyone even if she did hover constantly on the brink of an early and probably agonizing death. Assistance, when given by a poor sick creature, is always appreciated far more by the recipient than help offered by a robust person. To martyr herself was Diana's aim. She had, after all (she reminded everyone) accompanied Miss Lambe in the bathing machine, despite having a spot of the bronchials herself. Her being so afflicted and yet so obliging earned her excessive praise. Susan Parker seemed really to live in the shadow of Diana, and of the three Parkers who lived together in sickly bliss, she was the one most definitely prone to disease and the one least inclined to complain about it. Her sister, therefore, complained for her, her brother did not.

Sidney Parker, recently arrived in Sanditon from Eastbourne, was a young man Charlotte was eager to acquaint fully with. Their brief meeting on his arrival had been followed by a promise of assembling later that day. He came for dinner at Trafalgar House, which went off very well. But, according to Sidney Parker's view of things, better acquaintance was made later during the party's respite in the drawing room. "For," he announced, "one can never really get to know a person during a situation that begins with hors d'oeuvres and ends with raspberry fool, and Heaven forbid and Lord help us all, should a fish course prevail somewhere between these two then all chance of proper conversation is lost." In keeping with the sentiments of those who live by the sea, fish was considered, in the Parker household, the very basis of a staple diet.

"Have I ever told you, Miss Heywood," said Mr. Parker during dinner, "that our Sanditon fish is the finest in the world! I always urge Mrs. Parker to order a main course of fish. Our cook will, as a rule, try to sell us the idea of meat, she is a great one for a heavy meal, but I cannot wrench myself from a good local fish. In the summer, at least, I think it is to be recommended for its lightness. And we do not just restrict to the sea, our rivers team with gifts for the table, our salmon with shrimp sauce is a perpetual delight and often better received than a chicken."

"I consider fish the most antisocial dish one can offer, especially where new acquaintance must be made," observed Sidney with a smile.

"My brother, Miss Heywood, laughs at everything, I think I warned you," cried Mr. Parker with joviality.

"Fish is no laughing matter when it comes to eating it," retorted Sidney, "one must have the knowledge of an anatomist and the skill of a surgeon to procure a small mouthful, I see no humor in that! What kind of meal is it that ends half in frustration and half in starvation?" He turned to Miss Heywood, who was seated next to him, and said, with every intention of making her easy, "I see a bone like a dagger in your fillet, Miss Heywood, pray do not swallow it."

Charlotte laughed. "I shall take heed of your advice, Sir."

They were in no such danger in the drawing room. The wine was safe to drink, according to Sidney, the coffee a tolerably good blend, and the company pleasing. This last Charlotte knew to be directed at her, and Sidney Parker proved her case by paying her every attention, leading the conversation with particulars of his family.

"My sisters and poor Arthur are come into Sanditon I understand! Well there is a surprise. They never venture anywhere, Miss Heywood; they stay mostly at home, indoors. Away from light and germs and *life*! They live quietly, devotedly, with the express purpose of convincing my poor impressionable brother Arthur that he is at death's door. My family, you will soon learn, has not a steady member amongst it!"

"Sidney!" exclaimed his sister-in-law.

"My sister-in-law is inclined to think me too harsh," he confided, "but, I speak the truth, my brother here is quite demented over Sanditon, and my other relatives are quite demented about sickness, you would think, would you not, Miss Heywood, that between them some cures might be discovered?"

Miss Heywood smiled. "Your disapproval is too affectionate to be taken seriously. You clearly love your poor family and no doubt talk of them incessantly whenever you can. But you have given me quite enough details of them and none of yourself, by what means am I to make out your character?" said she.

"I am sure my brother here has given you particulars," this with a warm smile to Mr. Parker, "my fault, if he is to be believed, is that I scoff at everything, apparently, and ... "

Mr. Parker interjected with good humor. "I confess I have already described you as a saucy fellow to Miss Heywood," he said. "The description befits you Sidney, you will not deny it, will you?"

Sidney laughed. "I dare not. You are quite fixed in your thinking. A saucy fellow, eh? How am I to live up to this expectation?"

"I do not foresee too much difficulty, Sir," said Charlotte. "You seem to qualify for the title."

Sidney Parker stood up, his feigned indignation at the affront serving very well to prove him something of a performer, a dramatist. He was a man who favored big gestures, exaggerations, and comedic turns.

"You have shocked me, Miss Heywood," cried he, with a flourishing hand to his heart. "In truth, if I were less well-mannered, I should be inclined to call you a saucy girl!"

Ease and affability defined their discourse. Sidney Parker had about him the confidence of one who has no financial worries and the cool poise of a man who has the acumen to ensure he never will have. His jovial manner and propensity to jest about everything meant others were easy in his company. He was not all frivolity though, he simply preferred this stance. "In truth, Miss Heywood, someone has to be an easy sort of fellow in this family, Heaven help us!" he exclaimed.

With happy thoughts of the day passed Charlotte retired to bed. Was she becoming taken up with Sanditon? The sound of the sea at night, the gulls' screeches in the morning, and the peculiar inhabitants—she would miss it all when she left. The mysteries unfolding were temptation enough for her to wish to extend her stay. Intrigue kept her awake; what conquests lay ahead for Sir Edward Denham? The Miss Beauforts? Both of them? Shocking thought! Charlotte could not clearly ascertain who was the hunter and who was the prey in that situation. It was certain though that the pursuit would be savage and the results likewise. She began, with a feeling of determination, to want to know all Miss Brereton's news. Unanswered questions frustrated her.

Happy, valuable, beneficial Sanditon with its sparkling sea and its cloudless skies. Was it so unsullied as she was to believe? Her sleep that night was fitful, her dreams lucid and unsettling: Sir Edward Denham was whispering in her ear again, the Miss Beauforts hid their smirking faces behind their fans, and Sidney Parker was laughing, while a girl she did not recognize danced a jig along the promenade holding a soup ladle.

CHAPTER 14

Charlotte Heywood's natural inclination to observe the Sanditon inhabitants was soon to be satisfied. For what better situation is there than a garden party to afford so analytical a creature so perfect an opportunity for observation. It was quite decided upon. They would be blessed with good weather, and of guests there would be no shortage. The grounds of Trafalgar House lent themselves exceedingly well to such an event, and the party would, naturally, go off well. *This* was Sanditon! Mrs. Parker, although quite capable and perfectly content to make all the arrangements, was obliged to accept Miss Diana Parker's offers of assistance. *She* could draw up a list of the afternoon's activities, although a recent attack of bowel inflammation left her disinclined to rush about the place.

"But Mary, let me put your mind at ease," Diana said weakly, "I shall be quite equal to taking on lists so long as my family's health allows it. You know I cannot focus my mind to any task without a list. I am one who is quite unanchored without an inventory."

Lady Denham accepted the invitation. "Of course you shall have me there, Mrs. Parker, but I must insist upon having that spot beneath your canvas awning as my own. I dehydrate in direct sun ... brain shrinkage is a very real danger at my age. My poor dear husband," it was not clear to which poor dear husband she referred, "would very likely have lived longer had he shielded his head from the heat," said she.

Mr. Sidney Parker was, quite as his brother had described him, a man full of joviality. His nieces and nephews loved him. Mrs. Parker often complained that her brother-in-law overindulged her four little ones but Sidney was unstoppable. He bought the children theatrical masks, he made paper ships, he told the most interesting stories, all invented and all with something fantastic in them, and he wrote their names, and his own, backwards, to make them laugh.

There was something rather admirable, Charlotte thought, about a man who could see the entertainment of children as valuable. There was no such desire to run and laugh and amuse in Mr. Parker, he had fathered and he loved his children, but it was always Sidney (Uncle "Yendis") who was responsible for laughter.

There were daily conversations between Sidney Parker and Charlotte Heywood. Having found themselves obliged to stay in the same house, these regular talks became something of a habit. Sidney, eager to remove from the stifling gentility of the lodgings he had taken on the Terrace, fixed himself with every intention of permanence at Trafalgar House. His view, that breakfasts, lunches, teas, and suppers all require a garnish of talk to make them tolerable, was demonstrated by his incessant conversation and his apparent inability to remain silent, even when the encumbrance of a fish was to be considered.

"There is nothing so grating on the nerves as the constancy of silence and the sound of a spoon on a dish. The clink of cup against a saucer drives me quite wild. I must have talk!" said Sidney.

"Does gossip satisfy you then? Would you not favor silence if the only talk to be had were mediocre, idle?" asked Charlotte.

"No, Madam, I certainly should not. Quiet simply blasts my ears. I should infinitely prefer idle talk to none at all."

"But you would not take it seriously?"

"Certainly not. But must everything be serious, Miss Heywood? I often see you hiding a smile or two."

"That is, perhaps, merely a girlish habit. One which you are unlikely to be prone to."

Diana Parker's list making proved something of a task. Details of the catering alone covered four sheets of pressed paper. She did not want picnic food! She did not want a banquet. She had settled upon something in-between. The entertainments were perplexing her; Sidney suggested Bullet Pudding for the children, Diana threw her hands up in dismay, and Mrs. Parker finally squashed the idea by telling a dreadful story of a choked child. There were to be card games and, (this too was Sidney's idea) the possibility of a Masquerade was discussed. "I heard they had one at Ranelagh," said he, "and it went off terribly well. The entire garden filled with masks. It would be vastly funny."

"Trafalgar House, fine though it is, is not quite Ranelagh, Sidney," said Diana wearily, "we must tailor our plans accordingly, besides, I so dislike masks, there is something fearsome in them. It vexes me not to know a person, not to see who they are."

"Then you must spend your life in a state of vexation, sister," said Sidney, "for no one shows themselves fully. We are all masqueraders to some degree."

"And what guise do you adopt, Sir?" said Charlotte, surprised.

"Why that of your commonplace jester, Miss Heywood, but I have a solemn side. Never mistake me for nothing more than a comedian. I have what might be termed a fluctuating tendency toward gravity. I can frown as hard as the next men when it is required of me."

"I do not think I ever saw you somber. There is nothing tragic or grave in you. You do laugh at life, at everything."

"Outwardly yes, but I am not all mirth. I have not grinned my way about the world. After a man is one and twenty he must honor the expectation of being mature. You might not believe it, Miss Heywood, but I am quite capable of proper feeling."

"Perhaps though, Sir, you are not so capable of showing it," said Charlotte.

Diana Parker's insistence that costumes and masks were not to be considered halted their conversation sharply. They must focus on the practicalities; this they, Charlotte and Sidney, did accordingly but there was something altered in the way they now saw each other. Sidney was unmasking, and Charlotte, whose openness was one of her admirable points, was inclined to shield herself. She was not sure, or perhaps could not acknowledge, that her feelings for Sidney Parker had advanced, changed. She was privately concerned that she was falling in love with him. The danger, however, of falling in love with such a lighthearted fellow, might be very great. She would therefore enjoy his company but view him with caution. She was not to be drawn in.

Chapter 15

All the neighborhood of Sanditon was deserted on the afternoon of the garden party. Mrs. Whitby had closed the library, Mr. Heeley had, reluctantly, locked the door of his shop, with the full belief that doing so would disappoint any young lady enamored with the idea of blue shoes. He had sold one pair to Miss Letitia Beaufort and another to her sister. The prospect of the garden party had also boosted Mr. Jebb's business and he found himself quite willing to shut shop once the very last bonnets and parasols had been purchased.

Residents and visitors in their entirety crowded into the gardens of Trafalgar House. A day's respite and the opportunity to consume cold cordial, wine, and all manner of delicacies in abundance attracted even those personages who rarely ventured out of doors. Mr. Parker had prepared a speech. The advantage of having such an audience must be put to good use. Promotion of Sanditon being his subject matter, he set himself upon a podium of wood to address his guests. To be so pinnacled, he thought, with a surge of pride, suited him very well and from his elevated position, he noted how obliging the Sanditon citizens all appeared.

The whole of the garden, when viewed from this heady peak, could be taken in and a good view of the amassed guests could be had. Mrs. Mathews and her three daughters had been amongst the first to arrive and were soon engaged in a lively conversation with Mr. Richard Pratt. Lieutenant Smith and Captain Little were rallying around Mrs. Jane Fisher and her daughter; and a Mrs. Scroggs, only recently widowed, was accompanied by the Reverend Hanking. Her muslin was newly dyed and she wore a mourning ring but her somber attire did little to disguise her delight at being out and about. It was suspected that the loss of her husband had been long awaited and welcomed. She seemed a heartily happy woman, one who, despite her recent bereavement, thought nothing of admiring one gentleman's shooting jacket. There was, in her opinion, something indefinably attractive about country attire.

It is certainly a good turnout, thought Mr. Parker spotting Mr. Beard, the solicitor from Grays Inn, who waved and said, "Mrs. Davis and Miss Merryweather are to join me later, Mr. Parker, but a headache keeps Mrs. Davis inside until after midday."

"Oh dear," said Mr. Parker, "but I'll shall rely upon seeing them, no one suffers a headache any longer than is necessary, at least not here in Sanditon. You know an ache of any sort cannot not long continue its assault to the body in such a corrective environment."

All the visitors whose names had been first known to Mr. Parker from the library listings were present. His interest, however, was in one Dr. Brown. Mr. Parker very clearly recalled seeing his name listed. The doctor and his wife were to arrive a little late and looking a little flustered.

"I hope our good hill has not exhausted you, Sir," said Mr. Parker stepping from the podium onto the grass.

"Not at all, Sir, we, my wife and I," this with a gesture toward the lady beside him, "find hill walking quite exhilarating. After London, Sir, such endeavors are a treat. I have even purchased sturdy boots for the purpose."

Next came the matter of formal introduction. Dr. Brown, an elderly man with a stooped posture, learned of Mr. Parker's desire to establish a medical practice in the neighborhood.

"I am not your man, Sir! I have retirement in my view. I no longer have the steadiness of hand or the good eyesight I once did. Hence this little seaside break. I can scarce apply a cup these days. London has had all of me. Indeed, it has had the best of me. My wife pleads for me to stop. For a man who has enjoyed good health all of his life I have spent a great deal of my time in infirmaries." To this his wife added nothing more than, "Too much time."

Brown, then, was not Sanditon's much-needed doctor, but Mr. Parker's disappointment did not live long. Willingden Abbots was always in his mind.

Sir Edward Denham had not arms enough to satisfy his desires. Having five young ladies with whom he intended to flirt meant that two arms proved to be three deficient of his needs. He started about the grounds with the Miss Beauforts dangled about him. Their choice of finery far exceeded anything that they had been seen in thus far. Their fans, Charlotte noticed, had been cast aside in favor of parasols. More lace than a haberdasher could hold bedecked their pretty sunshades. Jebb's was certain to have empty shelves the following day. Sir Edward, firmly bound betwixt these two with their umbrellas, was entirely possessed and without chance of escape. The threesome passed by Charlotte, the two outer smiled, he in the middle could not bow for the constraint his feminine captors put upon him, but he affected a nod in her direction. He was engaged in matters poetic, as was his expected mode of flirtation. "O, that I were a glove upon that hand," said he when one of the Miss Beauforts put a delicate finger to her cheek.

Arthur Parker was quite settled in a chair by the picnic table, giving an account of his ill health to Lieutenant Smith, whose appearance of compassion gave no clue to his rather unkind intention of later regaling his seafaring colleagues with tales of the fleshy, feeble young man who sat before him.

"I must always ensure that I have adequate nourishment in the heat," said Arthur, "liquid does nothing to improve me, I must insist on substance; when I have a little bread, cold cuts perhaps, and something in the way of cake I find am almost as fit as the next man. My sisters, they are natural nurses the both of them, worry a great deal for my health. They keep it in their mind that I must consider foodstuffs a danger, and yet I always find myself healthier when I have not been deprived. I cannot starve. I am always the worse for an empty stomach." Of his new acquaintance he inquired, "Does not the sea unsteady you, Sir?" Neither expecting nor waiting for an answer he went on, "I confess to envying your constitution, I fear I would be quite hopeless aboard ship, firstly, I am intolerant of too much movement and secondly, my sisters tell me I cannot swim, though I have to admit I am not sure that I have ever tried. Immersion is a mystery to me. That, Sir, is the long and the short of it, but then women do fuss so, do you not agree?"

Lieutenant Smith was a sensible hardwearing young man of about five and twenty who laughed and said, "A certain type of woman may fuss if allowed to do so but it is not solely a feminine quality. I know more than a handful of gentlemen given to fluster at trivialities. One such survives on nothing more than the odd boiled egg, eaten cold, and even that must be of a particular size. I need not mention that these worriers are *not* sailors. We seafarers are, as you rightly point out, blessed with a tolerance, with a particular strength of constitution. But it is not to be envied, I assure you. With every advantage, there must come a penalty, and mine is that I am almost as repelled by dry land as you are by the idea of the swells of the ocean, Sir. I manage tolerably well here," this last with a stamp of his foot and sweep of his hand, "where the sea is at my disposal for bathing. I set sail again next spring and the moment cannot come soon enough."

"But the confinement of your ships!" cried Arthur. "I think only of cramped cabins and the proximity of so many other men. It must prove unsociable to some degree."

"You are quite mistaken, Sir," said Lieutenant Smith. "The restriction of space, I grant you, is often resented, but superior camaraderie like that found amongst sailors cannot be so marked in any other set of men in the world. I assure you I would rather spend a Rope Yarn Sunday aboard ship than suffer too many drawing rooms or too many games of écarté."

The Parker sisters complained of the humidity. "Oh, what it is to be frail, Susan," said Diana Parker. "I feel quite unequal to the heat myself but I fear more for *you* sister, your constitution might not take well to this oppressive climate. It would be as well to have the leeches this evening."

The four Parker children ran about the grass at a game of cup and ball. Sidney Parker, the only relative who thought himself in good enough health to be of consequence to the Parker brood, chased after his nephews and nieces, roaring and laughing. Mrs. Parker worried for her flock, that their high spirits might inconvenience those of a less tolerant nature.

"Hush children! Sidney, calm the children, they are quite without reason when you get the idea to entertain them. No, Sidney! *Please*! They are frenzied enough and it shall not be you who is obliged to settle them. To think that you had the idea of letting them play at Bullet Pudding. Do you see now how wild they get? Pray think of a quiet game. Poor creatures, they are, all four of them, little Mary especially, quite breathless as it is. I dread to think what perils might befall them if I allowed you your way."

Sidney took leave of his nephews and nieces. Their protestations could not dissuade him. "Your dear mama has it that you are frenzied little beasts, we must desist, a quiet game later perhaps."

He was soon by Charlotte, with the formalities of greeting each other attended to, their conversation slipped easily into matters general.

"Where is Miss Brereton today?" asked she.

"I imagined she was with Lady Denham, but I do not see her now I seek to, she must be taking a turn, she is a great one for turns you know."

"Yes she is, she regularly walks alone by Sanditon House, she told me herself."

"Oh I doubt she is ever too much alone, a pretty example like Miss Brereton rarely exemplifies solitude," replied Sidney, and chancing to glance toward the perimeters of the grounds saw the very young lady they had just engaged in conversation about. "I take back what I said, Miss Heywood, Miss Clara Brereton *is* the very picture of solitude this afternoon. See there, walking the orchard, is it not Miss Brereton?" Charlotte saw amongst the trees the solitary figure and knew it to be Clara.

"Yes it is her, should we imagine she walks that way to signify loneliness in order that she will be taken pity on and joined in her walk, or is her desire for isolation genuine, do you think?"

"Heavens above!" cried Sidney with a laugh. "I had not in all the world imagined so deep an analysis could be applied to a girl's decision to walk alone."

"One of my many faults," said Charlotte. "I am inclined to see mystery in everything and sense in nothing."

Sidney Parker offered Charlotte his arm. "Walk with me, Miss Heywood, make of it what you will, a curiosity or a nonsense, your judgment will have no effect on the pleasure it will give me to escort you."

If Sidney Parker's intention had been to bestow his attentions only on Miss Heywood, he was soon to have his plans thwarted, for they had not yet walked the circumference of the lawn when Clara Brereton came upon them and Sidney was obliged to have her at his left side while Charlotte was on his right. That the parade was a comical reflection of Sir Edward Denham's alliance with the Miss Beauforts was an idea that instantly occurred to Charlotte. Before long the Denham threesome passed the Parker group, the Miss Beauforts giggled, and the gentlemen began some civilities; the weather, sport, business, all manner of subjects were covered.

"It seems quite the trend to escort two ladies these days, Sidney," said Sir Edward with good humor.

"I concede, it is a fashion I imagine will take off," said Sidney in response.

Edward Denham smiled. "It saves the trouble of choosing! For what sane man can make a distinction between two examples of beauty? I am notoriously bad at coming to decisions, this way I need make none."

Charlotte seized the moment. "It is not such an uncommon sight, Sir Edward. It brings to my mind a vivid memory of a very senior gentleman being taken around an exhibition by two young ladies. The story, as I recall it, was that the gentleman was in some way infirm or unstable and the two young ladies had taken pity on him."

Sir Edward Denham laughed and gestured toward the Miss Beauforts who were still clinging to him. "'Twould be a pretty pity though, do you not agree?"

CHAPTER 16

The events of the afternoon unfolded in something of an expected manner. The heat increased and with it Arthur Parker's appetite. Lady Denham had begun to feel fatigued by the time Tom Parker was alighted upon his podium with his speech polished and ready to be heard.

Latecomers to such events are always greeted with unwarranted excitement. This enthusiasm often bears no relation to the person's having unusual qualities or outstanding gifts; it is merely their lack of punctuality that affords them undue allure. Miss Esther Denham was so regularly late that there was a kind of reliability about her. It was her absolute abhorrence to arrive at a place without there being the highest possibility of her being seen by everyone. The aspect of herself that she most eagerly wished to draw attention to was her devotion. Lady Denham had a dependency on devotion, but she was not so foolish as to think that Miss Denham's compassionate attentions were all the result of concern. Such love, such care as the kind Miss Denham bestowed upon her senior relative was outwardly impressive but inwardly calculating. A share of the lady's fortune governed every smile, every errand, every benevolent offer to read aloud to or otherwise entertain her aunt. Miss Denham was always supremely attentive to Lady Denham but an audience could be depended upon to improve the manner and the depth of her commitment. If Lady Denham's Sanditon neighbors could all see what a good-hearted, deserving girl Miss Denham was, then they were sure to recommend her as being so.

Lady Denham's fortune was no secret, but the nature of her intentions for it was. No hint of her proposals ever left her lips and those three parties, the Denhams, the Hollises and Miss Brereton, who considered themselves likely contenders for it, vied with each other in the sweetest of ways. Sir Edward and Miss Denham had formed a kind of alliance; it was very likely, they thought, that one or the other would be favored, their shared name and relationship would ensure security for both. But there hung around this arrangement an uneasy feeling that on acquisition of the fortune, the favored party might well forget all previous promises of generosity.

What a monstrous dictator money is! It forces civility between foes, creates acrimony between supposed friends, and has been the cause of countless loveless marriages throughout the world. It is hard to say, of this little circle of contenders, which member was the most calculating or self interested and harder still to say which the most probable recipient of the coveted riches. And it was almost impossible to find any one of the competitors entirely deserving. The Denhams were concerned that Clara Brereton, by the nature of her constancy and general sweetness, might just succeed. The Hollises' chances did not seem great, they were rarely come to Sanditon, and it was hoped, by Miss Brereton and the Denhams alike, that their absence would make them as good as forgotten. A sudden visit by the Hollises was dreaded, the avoidance of informing them, should Lady Denham fall ill, was agreed upon between Sir Edward and his sister; in this their complicity was unreserved. Where Miss Denham was scheming, her brother was thrice so, and accepting there to be a likelihood of Miss Brereton's inheriting, the pair had devised a plan to ensure that he could ingratiate himself to her. Love, or the cunning imitation of such emotion, was his favored weapon in what he acknowledged to be a battle. Sir Edward Denham, having decided that softening of Miss Brereton by way of emotional manipulation would be his security, did not appear to be making a success of things. He actively pursued other ladies, overtly flattered them, even in Miss Brereton's presence, and flirted without restraint at every given opportunity with the first woman unfortunate enough to give him a polite smile. Could Miss Brereton think him so in love with her and believe herself to be similarly enamored with him when all his actions seemed to imply otherwise? She did not question it. She did not give consequence to the fervent attentions he showed to any lady who came into the neighborhood. She barely acknowledged him, crushed between the Miss Beauforts, and there seemed, in her denial of his presence, no malice, no hurt pride, nor any feelings of rejection.

Charlotte's introduction to Miss Denham was brief, for the latter was eager to be by Lady Denham immediately. "Forgive me, Miss Heywood, I have been quite determined to make your acquaintance but Lady Denham looks fatigued, does she not? I must forego any chance of starting a conversation and go to her at once, excuse me."

Lady Denham was tiring and despite her own avid interest and ample investment in Sanditon was unable to sustain prolonged enthusiasm for Mr. Parker's promotional speech. She was not given to fainting, she had never been a swooner, not even in her youth, so her collapse had about it the appeal that novelties invariably bring. The vapors were called for, and once they had been administered and praised for their remarkable effectiveness, Lady Denham was thereafter escorted home to Sanditon House. One nurse is usually considered equal to the task of attending one patient, but Lady Denham was obliged to accept the attention of three aids. Clara Brereton, Miss Denham, and Sir Edward all departed with expressions of gravity and very powerful feelings of anticipation.

The Miss Beauforts expounded between themselves on the inconvenience of having lost their admirer so early in the afternoon and knowing Sidney Parker to be handsome but otherwise engaged they deigned to grace his brother Arthur with their company. He was not the handsomest of men (the Miss Beauforts loved a handsome admirer) but he would do in place of any other. Poor Arthur was forced to talk! This he managed between mouthfuls. He had never enjoyed female attention other than that of his sisters, to be enjoying it now from two young ladies was a marvel to him. They giggled when he spoke and sometimes when he did not. Arthur took their laughter to be a measure of his success in the art of amusing the fairer sex, so he spoke more and ate less.

Diana was concerned for her sickly brother's well-being. "He should not over enthuse, he will be sure to suffer later, all manner of irregularities will no doubt seize him. Not that I wish to shield poor Arthur from social pleasures, no, indeed I do not, but it will fall to me to resurrect his health, I am quite harsh upon myself in matters of duty. But I am far from robust, that is no secret, and Arthur is prone to an internal condition, that is something of a delicate matter and I worry terribly. But it does not end there. We are quite stricken as a group. My sister Susan, of course, is entirely reliant on the leeches. Cupping has no effect on her. Wet or dry. It is completely ineffectual! It must always be leeches for Susan, but she is so reluctant to give up her blood that three are applied to draw just an ounce from her. The best I can hope for, for myself, after such an afternoon, is that some bitters will be my salvation. If I manage some bread that alone will be a miracle." All this she voiced to Mrs. Whitby who heard the forthright declarations with astonishment. She had been sitting with Miss Lambe whose appearance at the gathering had had less effect than Mrs. Griffiths would have liked and far more than the girl herself would have wished for.

"It is a shame, my dear, that Sir Edward Denham has departed," said Mrs. Griffiths to her charge. "I rather hoped that your acquaintance with him would be enlarged upon this afternoon."

CHAPTER 17

Every neighborhood should have a great lady. If that great lady should faint away at a garden party, then the garden party must be deemed to be over. Mr. Parker did not complete his speech, Miss Lambe could not enjoy Sir Edward Denham's overtures, and all manner of little things could not take place. Guests departed and as the day drew to a close only the Parker family members and the servants remained. The Parker children had quite exhausted themselves and were taken, for an early rest, into the house. Mr. and Mrs. Parker were likewise fatigued but satiated. Sidney had not left Charlotte's side for a moment. The afternoon had been theirs. They had walked, sat, talked, and laughed together. He engaged himself with unguarded freedom of expression and she with care. Only the brief moments when Miss Brereton had been in their company were they not alone. Mr. Parker, seeing his brother alone once Miss Heywood had gone to dress for dinner, took the opportunity of inquiring, with brotherly concern, about Sidney's motives.

"Motives?" cried Sidney. "Can a gentlemen not pay attention to a young lady without there being motives? Everything with you must be calculated. You have it that everyone has a scheme."

"Dear brother, do not be affronted, you know as well as I that undivided attention such as you have bestowed upon Miss Heywood is often thought to be indicative of a particular regard and all history has it that a proposal is usually made thereafter. I will not be the only one expecting an engagement."

Sidney laughed. "There is only one solution then if I am to save Sanditon from scandal," said Sidney.

His brother smiled. "You have it right, Sidney, you must pay attention to other young ladies, you may well favor Miss Heywood, brother, but it would be unreasonable to give the wrong impression. These little things are not to be taken lightly, these days so many young women are hankering for expediency where matrimony is concerned."

"I have no intention of paying attention to other young ladies," said Sidney sharply, "what is done is done! If I have encouraged Miss Heywood, or anyone else, to believe that I am to propose to her, then propose I must!"

The heat meant that Charlotte, in her room directly above where the brothers conversed in the garden, had opened the casement for air. The first of the conversation, she had not heard, but this next she caught clearly.

"You mean to propose to *Miss Heywood*! You have not known her but a moment Sidney, must you treat everything as a joke, must you laugh even at love and marriage?"

"Why not? What better way to approach the subject of matrimony than with a little merriment, it makes a good contrast, in my opinion, to the possible miseries that may thereafter ensue in wedlock! No! I cannot take any subject too seriously, I shall ask Miss Heywood to become my wife, and she will no doubt laugh as much I do. She enjoys a joke. There Tom, never let it be said that I do nothing to promote this place. You will have a wedding at Sanditon!"

Charlotte could not move from her spot by the window. To receive a proposal of marriage from a man who meant only to jest was more insulting to her than the prospect of never receiving one. "Deplorable conceit, to think that I would join in the joke and marry for no other reason than to create amusement," thought Charlotte. "And his conviction that I will accept! '*...you will have a wedding at Sanditon!'* There will not be such, not if am expected to be the bride. Oh! In what manner does he intend to propose that he thinks will induce me to accept him? No doubt his ideas for the trousseau will include masks and a harlequin costume. Whatever his attitude, I shall refuse him."

Mr. Parker's immediate action was to inform his wife of Sidney's intentions in order that between the two of them they might, in as natural a way as could be achieved, leave Sidney and Miss Heywood alone together in order that the proposal could take place. They viewed the matter with the utmost gravity. A wedding would be a commercial success, a promotion, something of an attraction. "If the proposal could be arranged to occur before dinner," insisted Mrs. Parker, "we will have the whole of the evening to celebrate. Of course there is the matter of Mr. Heywood's permission, to make it firm, but your brother sways from convention so often that I'm sure he can at least make his feelings known to Charlotte." They were both so confident of a happy outcome that the cook was called into the drawing room and extra wine ordered for the evening.

Charlotte, beginning now to wish Sanditon air to be as restorative as it was reputed to be, walked in the garden. After some minutes she knew someone to be behind her and hoped it would be one of the servants. It was not. Sidney was in evening dress. So somberly attired for such a joke, thought she. He was by her and upon his insistence that they sit together, she soon found herself seated, under the canopy that had failed to protect Lady Denham from the insufferable heat, with the object of her aggravation beside her. She knew it must happen, but when he took her hand in his, she found herself responding with discomfort. His voice was low, measured, with no sign of his usual joviality.

"My dear Miss Heywood, *Charlotte*," said he without hesitation, "as my brother was quick to remind me, I have barely known you a moment but believe me when I tell you I have longed for you for a lifetime, I concede this is sudden, amazing, maybe even ridiculous but I am impulsive and my impulse must be succumbed to. I cannot imagine your feelings for me have developed as rapidly as mine for you have done, but I feel confident that they will, in time, grow to equal proportions."

Charlotte had done nothing but stare at Sidney Parker and now, withdrawing her hand from his, she spoke, "By that I assume you mean that I will one day be inclined to see you as the object of *my* jokes."

"Miss Heywood?"

"Is that not what I am, Sir, an unfortunate, unwitting, and gullible object of ridicule?"

Sidney raised his voice. "No, Madam, this is not a joke! I am asking you to marry me."

Charlotte's anger could not be contained. "And do you presume, for some unfathomable reason of your own, that proposing in the mode of a fool will incite me to accept you?"

Sidney stood before her. "What part of my proposal makes you view me as a jester? I spoke with sincerity, Miss Heywood. When I said it may seem ridiculous I meant only that you might think me so, for being so little acquainted with you and yet so in love."

"Oh!" cried she astonished. "You are in love with me, are you? Your thoughts leap from mockery to tenderness with rapidity, Sir."

"Why do you think me insincere, Charlotte? Why do you reject me thus? If you do not love me nor think you can, be kinder than this and tell me so, but I beg you, do not torment me by suggesting that *my* feelings are in doubt."

Charlotte stood now. "Then, Sir, believe me when I say, I do not love you and I do not think I ever could!" Turning away from him she headed toward to the house. He called to her but she did not look back, she went straight to her room and did not come down for dinner. From her window she saw that Sidney stayed in the garden some time, until his brother went thither under the canopy to persuade him to go inside. The brotherly arm around the rejected shoulder, the slow dejected walk of the man she had refused awakened Charlotte to the idea that she might have misjudged Sidney. But had she not heard him in his own words describe the idea of marrying her as a joke?

Oh, what confusing creatures men were, his proposal, now she remembered it, was not jesting, not sarcastic in tone or light-hearted in any way. What had she done in refusing him? Many a woman has agreed to marry a man and regretted it fully by the next morning, but in refusing a man, how could a woman expect him to ask her again. Men were not inclined to invite rejection repeatedly, Charlotte knew enough about their temperaments to deduce that. "He is lost to me," she said quietly, "he who I loved, though I did not know it, he who I do love. I have denied all proper feeling and the damage is surely irreparable, I have told him I could never love him!"

CHAPTER 18

By morning Charlotte was ever more convinced that she was irrevocably in love with Sidney Parker, but to feel so with no means to express it was the cause of great despair. He had gone the previous evening to Eastbourne. Mr. and Mrs. Parker, maintaining their position as the kindest host and hostess the world could ever know, said not a word about the matter, both assuming, their opinion being based on Sidney's report, that she, Charlotte, felt nothing more than mildly perplexed. They had not the first idea of her being in love with Sidney and, as she was not about to reveal it when doing so seemed so pointless, they remained quite ignorant of the facts. Sidney was out of reach.

Reports of Lady Denham's health affirmed that she was still suffering from fatigue and would very likely be bedridden for some weeks. All this was reported by Diana Parker who, seizing the opportunity to be useful, had offered her services as soon as was possible. She was, as she made clear with regularity, quite strained enough herself with Arthur's recent decline; his irregularities, as she had predicted, had returned with astonishing reliability. Nevertheless, Diana Parker was inclined to let him recover by his own means, as his ailments, everyone agreed, had been brought about by his own means. "Too much excitement is never a good thing for the boy. He palpitates so."

A week had passed when some news came for Miss Lambe, which led to her departing Sanditon the next morning. Mrs. Griffiths, who abhorred the idea of seeing to the packing of trunks in haste, was more than a little vexed.

"Dresses never surrender neatly to folding when one is in a hurry."

Mr. Parker, who was also leaving that day, agreed to accompany Miss Lambe to Eastbourne. He had business in London to attend to and the intention of detouring to Willingden Abbots in order to resume his search for a doctor. The idea of bringing one of Charlotte's sisters back to Sanditon had not occurred to him and might not have done if it had not been for the letter Charlotte received from her father requesting that Abigail be allowed to join them there. With so much to do and so many places to go to Mr. Parker felt with renewed vigor that life was a true adventure. He was a crusader. Miss Lambe, he was told, must be deposited at Mrs. Griffiths's sister's house. Every effort must be made to keep the girl out of the way of drafts, even in the post chaise. Mrs. Griffiths gave the details of the address.

"My sister, she is lately married and become a Mrs. Cheveley, will receive the girl, I insist she stays a month, at least, for medical examinations. It pains me to lose her even temporarily but I must always have her best interests in my heart. I shall miss her, you know, for she never troubles me at all. She barely speaks two words together but she is the greatest listener. My husband, when he was alive, always maintained that I would run out of breath long before I ran out of words."

This last convinced Mr. Parker that he was not misleading himself about the presence of a doctor at Sanditon being beneficial, for if the patronage of such illustrious personages as Miss Lambe was to be secured by there being such a man present, then to the task of finding that man he must apply every last drop of his energies. The loss of Miss Lambe for a whole month represented an economic tragedy. But there was nothing to be done!

Mr. Parker set Miss Lambe right at Eastbourne, spending a full hour with Mrs. Cheveley, finding her a pleasing, if rather simple, woman. He spent a further hour with Sidney, the nature of this time could not be described as pleasant. Sidney, who was apt, in times past, to laugh at life, was sadly disinclined to do so now. His brother, as a means of bringing him to his senses, confessed that he detected no feelings of remorse on the side of Miss Heywood and advised that Sidney would be best recovered, and swiftly too, if he would only put the matter behind him. Thinking that there would be an end to the disappointment Mr. Parker went on to London to complete his business matters with his attorney and looked forward to his later endeavors which would take him back into his beloved Sussex to Willingden Abbots. There, he felt with utter conviction, he would come across the fine medical man of his dreams. It was his hope that Sidney, benefiting from the small measure of filial advice he had proffered, would soon be improved. How unlike himself he now appeared, how shadowy and hushed. Sidney, whose propensity was to burst into a room, had taken possession of the drawing room at the Sovereign Hotel with such an attitude of dejection as made him appear quite a stranger and it was there that his brother left him with very powerful feelings of concern.

Mr. Parker's meeting with his attorney, a Mr. Henry Waldegrave of Gracechurch Street, was not to be done with quickly. The two men were on such friendly terms that their mutual enjoyment of the conversation, it was decided, must be continued.

"I have ordered a fine dinner at my hotel. If you would care to join me, I would rather relish the opportunity of further discussion," said Mr. Parker, who had indeed secured for himself a comfortable position in the dining room at his boarding place, not too near the window as to catch the draft, but near enough to enjoy observing London life. Mr. Parker relished viewing such activity, it always served to reinforce his opinion that Sanditon, his very own dear Sanditon, was something peaceful, something not far off paradise and certainly superior to any other place. Mr. Waldegrave agreed to join him and the pair met but a few hours later at Mr. Parker's hotel as arranged. Not expecting to see the Hollises, Mr. Parker did not, at first, recognize them. William Hollis and his sisters Julia and Eliza instantly identified Mr. Parker and went to introduce themselves without delay. The brother, being the eldest, spoke first.

"Mr. Parker, *I say,* it is Mr. Parker, is it not? We were quite right, my dears, it *is* Mr. Parker of Sanditon. What brings you to London, Sir?"

"Oh!" cried Mr. Parker in surprise, "a matter of business only, I leave tomorrow so I am afraid our acquaintance shall be cut short, but I shall be sure to give intelligence to Lady Denham of my having seen you all. This is all so unexpected. Something of a coincidence, I . . ."

Julia Hollis interjected, "How is Lady Denham?"

Eager to expound upon his own plans and seeing the means to introduce the idea of them in response to the lady's question, Mr. Parker gave an alarming account of Lady Denham's health. "Madam, without wishing to distress you unduly I must report that Lady Denham is quite without strength, an afternoon's sun being the initial cause of her malady. Usually, a person would be quite recovered from such an ailment after a day and night's rest, but the poor soul is almost entirely without the natural vigor that usually defines her. She is, as you would imagine, receiving every attention from her dear niece Miss Brereton and Miss Denham and Sir Edward are, of course, devoted." Once these particulars were given Mr. Parker went on to inform the party of his plans for a medical man at Sanditon. William, Julia, and Eliza Hollis exchanged looks of consternation but Mr. Parker was so elated at having their attention that he scarcely noticed and immediately seized the opportunity to give particulars of the speech he had planned for the garden party. There was, after all, no point in wasting an audience.

It was all decided in a moment, the three Hollises agreed they would travel to Sanditon, their confessed motive was that of wishing to reacquaint themselves with the place. "Your report of Sanditon tells of so many changes, Mr. Parker, that we are hardly able to believe it. My sisters and I are determined to go in to Sussex to see for ourselves. The idea is quite fixed in our minds now."

Mr. Parker was gladdened by the apparent success of his promotion. "Oh, you will not be disappointed, Sir, ladies, I assure you, it is the very place to be, and of course you will be better able to assess Lady Denham's state of health when you see her. My sister Diana—I cannot for the life of me think if you have met her or not—is in the neighborhood, depend upon it she will apply herself to finding you good lodgings, the Terrace is the place."

And so it was settled, the Hollis party would reach Sanditon before Mr. Parker was able to return to explain their having met in London. He was still fiercely determined to make it to Willingden Abbots and, feeling that his journeying already had an air of fortuity about it, was certain that this attempt to get a professional man would prove successful.

CHAPTER 19

Willingden Abbots, was, as Mr. Heywood had described it, quite down in the weald. In contrast to the steep ascent of Willingden that had overturned his carriage some weeks previously, his curricle was forced to descend a rather dramatic incline to get him into the place. His inquiries, first to a passerby and second at a butcher's shop, about the whereabouts of the practice featured in the newspaper articles he still kept in his possession, took him to Seymour Lane. Certainly the houses there had about them the very appearance Mr. Parker had expected. The dwellings were neither too humble nor too grand, but with an evenness of fascia and a balanced landscape, these properties were just the style. "This must be the very place," said Mr. Parker retrieving the papers from his pocket book for confirmation. "Yes, I am certain of it."

A gentleman, leaving the fifth house along the row of six, attracted Mr. Parker's attention by doing so and the latter's eye was thereby drawn to a sign mounted by the front door. Nothing could suppress Mr. Parker's impatience and he went toward the said gentleman with eager ideas about an introduction and cried out so loudly that the poor man was rendered quite startled.

"Sir! My dear fellow," said Mr. Parker in a state of agitation, "am I right in assuming you to be ... " referring again to the advertisement, "one of these practitioners mentioned here? One of these very gentleman?" said he with a firm jab of his finger at the papers. Mr. Parker was disinclined to wait for the man's answer, he was now on the path with the gentleman, with the advantage of being able to read the sign which read: Dr. L. M. Kendall and Partner. "Pray tell me, which of the two are you? Dr. Kendall himself or the partner? I dare not hazard to guess the truth."

The gentleman, his opportunity to speak now found and grasped, replied, "I am the partner, Sir, or rather I was, for I believe the term implies there must be two practicing and this is not the case. I am afraid this notice may have misled you. I *was* in partnership, I held a secondary position you understand, with Dr. Kendall, the dissolution of which I assume you are familiar with since the publication of the advertisement."

"Indeed, I have all the information, I have studied these cuttings repeatedly," said Mr. Parker.

"I am Dr. Wellscott, the remaining partner, if you need attention I would be happy to open the surgery and attend you, my mission is not one of urgency, I can postpone my trip to town on your account, Sir." Mr. Parker thought better of claiming no particular ailment and decided that some attention to his ankle, despite its being quite restored, might be the best means of securing this invite. And such was the nature of their business discussion; Mr. Parker readily praised the excellence of his precious Sanditon, with his lower leg exposed and laid bare for the doctor's perusal. All was decided with expediency. Dr. Wellscott had been going that very morning to send a letter of inquiry to a practice he had lately learned of which was situated in a village in the north of England. The primary concern of his investigation was to ascertain if the surgeon there was, as he believed, in need of a partner. Happenstance had led Mr. Parker to Dr. Wellscott. It was fortuity indeed that he had come that very day. There was no persuasion needed.

Dr. Wellscott thought the coincidence of events to be a blessing. "Such a pleasing chance for me, Sir," he said. "The lease on this building is due to expire. It is common knowledge in the neighborhood that my departure is imminent. My patients are already seeking advice from a neighboring man. I admit, I was loathe to deposit myself so far into the north of the country, but, until presented with your proposition, I felt I had little choice in the matter."

A propensity for swiftness of decision, on Mr. Parker's side, and Dr. Wellscott's eagerness to establish himself more locally, meant that the two gentlemen were soon shaking hands upon an agreement. The former was to return to Sanditon that afternoon, his detour must not be forgot, there was still the journey to Willingden proper to be made, and the collection of Charlotte's sister Abigail to be seen to. Dr. Wellscott, quite enamored with all he had heard, was to arrive at Sanditon the following week.

"I will have in my company a maid servant, she will accompany me. I generally refer to her as my nurse although the arrangement came about due to a combination of factors. She is *not* truly a nurse, Mr. Parker, I dare not make any such boasts on her behalf, but she is bright enough and has a mind fit for learning, she can mix a paste, prepare a poultice, or concoct linctuses as well as any medical person might do. To have such an assistant is an invaluable asset in my line of business. The sick you know, are never satisfied unless prescribed some foul-smelling, evil-tasting, ineffectual remedy. I can never overlook these placebos, the seriously ill care nothing for them, but those who imagine themselves at risk of expiry really seem to consider these prescriptions a confirmation of the severity of their disorders. Now this can go no further, Sir, but I confess I have had Maisie, that is my nurse you understand, prepare compounds and elixirs that consist of nothing more than components you or I would consider those ordinary gardenstuffs that are consumed daily. Oh! The effects of such preparations on the afflicted are miraculous! Any random extract will do them and by any means; consumed, inhaled, occluded, the modes of administration are seemingly endless, and the patients entirely willing to try any, or in some cases, all of them."

Mr. Parker smiled. "I think I can guarantee, Sir, your first patients to be my very own sisters and younger brother! Each one of the three has given up entirely on medical assistance and they are all currently in favor of, what I call, self doctoring." He clapped his hands. "You are exactly the kind of fellow I had hoped for, Dr. Wellscott, exactly the kind. I shall have everything ready at Sanditon to ensure you a warm welcome, and of course the same applies to your nurse, she sounds something of a treasure."

"Indeed, she is, she is visiting the sick at present but you will soon enough acquaint with her at Sanditon. She is something of an enigma, there is very little known of her past. My involvement with her came about through Dr. Kendall. A year or so gone by Maisie was placed in an infirmary in London, Dr. Kendall saved her from the madhouse, Sir. Memory loss, nothing more, nothing less. Memory loss can give the appearance of madness in the sufferer. Kendall brought her here, thank the Lord; through his kindness she escaped the indignity of such an institution. You might conclude, Sir, that Dr. Kendall is a good man, and in doing so, you would be correct. Quite so, he is such a person. If it were not for him, Maisie's destiny would have been quite different. As it is, the girl, as I have already illustrated, has a fine little existence and a sweeter, more willing assistant you will not find. She keeps good hours, is thorough in her work, honest in spirit, and very well presented. She does put one in mind of a girl who has been in service but there we are, that remains a mystery, she cannot remember any of her own history whatsoever!"

CHAPTER 20

Mr. Parker was quick to calculate that by the same time the following week Sanditon would have no less than six new inhabitants. Two of these would be permanent: Dr. Wellscott and his nurse, Maisie; the others, the Hollises and Abigail Heywood, would be a welcome addition in terms of numbers.

Charlotte Heywood's features were, as seemed the defining factor in her family, fine but strong, being beautiful without fragility. There was a familial resemblance between the two sisters, but Abigail had more of youth in her looks, being the younger by three years. She was happy to see Mr. Parker again and made polite inquiries about the progress of his ankle, since his injuring it at Willingden had been the means of their introduction. Almost the very same narrative as he had used to divert Charlotte during her first journey into Sanditon he now employed as a method of entertaining and informing her younger sister. Her parents, Mr. and Mrs. Heywood, had not altered and could not have been expected to. Despite Mr. Parker, once again, attempting to induce them to partake of Sanditon they would not be prevailed upon. There was always a reason, always something in the way of a country obligation, for them to stay close to their own hearth.

By the time their travels had taken them to Sanditon, Abigail Heywood had been well informed by Mr. Parker and felt herself to be as intimately acquainted as anyone could be with a place without having actually set foot in it.

The amount of premeditation that went into Sir Edward Denham's farewell was great indeed, for he knew he must bid adieu to

Clara Brereton, the Miss Beauforts, and Miss Heywood in a manner that would encourage them to mourn his absence. Sir Edward Denham could not bear to be absent and disregarded. His departure to London, he declared, had been planned some months. If the Miss Beauforts were dejected at the thought of his absence, Charlotte was not.

"I shall not grieve for want of him." To grieve for want of another was so much her occupation that to give even the slightest consideration to Sir Edward Denham was beyond her. Departures! Was every soul to rush away on a whim? She imagined Sanditon as a deserted remedial paradise. Sidney and Miss Lambe were in Eastbourne, together. It was certain that Miss Lambe was already being attended to by Sidney, was it not? His courteous nature would not allow him to overlook her. Rebounding love might be the impetus to spur Sidney toward pretty Miss Lambe. She might not be so readily diverted by his jokes as Charlotte had been, but she would no doubt bewitch him with her demure little nods. Frustration bit at Charlotte's senses, she had not been aware that her design was to procure a husband, had she not denied it with fervor to Mrs. Parker? How different this very day would be if she had taken Sidney at his word. "He was serious and I responded by insulting him, he must despise me; he must think me frivolous," thought she.

There was rarely a period of solitude when Charlotte did not recollect Sidney's proposal. This memory was her ghost, the shadow that threatened eternal possession of her thoughts. She berated herself. How easily she could have answered yes, how simple it would have been to declare her tenderness if she had not first opened her window that evening. Without a preconceived notion of any joke, she would never have presumed the intention to have been that of comedy. Were not his words and his countenance the very likeness of truth? *I spoke with sincerity, Miss Heywood, when I said it may seem ridiculous I meant only that you might think me so, for being so little acquainted with you and yet so in love.* Love *she* had induced and then extinguished. For want of a little less pride she might have responded differently. "I was prejudiced against him from the very start, his natural inclination to amuse and see the amusing was what I took to be his entire nature," she thought. Am I so blind? Can I have been so irrational as to think the jester his only role? Why did I not recall his words: *Never mistake me for nothing more than a comedian*. It was insufferable. She had rejoiced in knowing him, in finding a kindred heart so certain to fill her own, in meeting with a mind designed so perfectly to adjoin hers. She had forfeited love for the sake of being forthright. From a fatuous determination to be wilful, opinionated, and impenetrable came her loneliness and her complete despair. "I do not want to live in the world dreading the risk of hearing that he has married," thought she, "the pain of suffering news of his having a family I shall fear all my days. I could never respond kindly to such intelligence, no amount of lifetimes could transport me far enough away from memories of him to allow me to feel generosity. Oh! But how I wish to, how calmed my poor heart is at the thought of him, no acrimony resides there, no resentment, but regret has withered my spirit. I have loved, I must resign to it. I *do* love, but have relinquished the object of my affections because of pure imprudence. My love is so abundant, so replete as to consume all areas of my affection; there is not the smallest space that another could fill."

In such cases as Charlotte's, the confidence of a sister is often considered the best place to lay troubles and Abigail Heywood, if a little fatigued from her journey and from Mr. Parker's enthusiastic account of Sanditon, had never been so happy to see her sister and had never been so surprised by her appearance.

"Oh my goodness! I was prepared for you to appear quite altered by your time at the coast, Charlotte, but I confess an improvement was expected." This last was delivered with sisterly concern.

Charlotte defended herself. "I am quite well, Abigail, a little pale today but I think perhaps you have been too readily influenced by Mr. Parker's declarations of Sanditon. If you came in anticipation of a dramatic change in me, then I fully comprehend your disappointment. Sea air is no miracle."

"No, Charlotte, you do not disappoint me, but I admit I had expected to find you … happier."

It could not be concealed. Charlotte could master suppression of her feelings with the good citizens of Sanditon, but from her sister's eye, the truth could not be hid and must be owned outright. When all the necessary introductions had all been made, the two went to Charlotte's room where the latter described the events leading to Sidney's proposal.

Abigail, being still young, was at times distracted by the romanticism of her sister's story and she leapt up from the bed at one point to ask irrelevant questions with inappropriate curiosity.

"Was it from this very window here that you heard him?"

Charlotte, all heartache and irritation, implored her young sister, "I wish to keep to the facts, have some heart, it pains me enough to recall the situation without my feeling it necessary to reenact the parts you favor, we are not at the theater, Abigail!"

"Oh, Charlotte, you mistake me, I do not mean to make light of your distress, but it is somewhat farcical, is it not?"

"To you, Abigail, it may well seem to be. You know I like to laugh whenever I can but I confess that in this matter all humor is lost to me."

"Please say you are not angry with me though?"

The sisters were not long aggrieved with one another and the younger, despite her natural disposition dictating otherwise, was soon to find enough sympathy to appease the elder. That sympathy was neither sought nor received readily on Charlotte's part did not lessen the fact that it had been genuinely given. To relate her distress and the causes of it afforded Charlotte a degree of relief and she was soon better able to indulge her sister by telling her about the good people of Sanditon. To Abigail this was delight itself.

"How exciting. I should dearly love to meet this Sir Edward!" cried she.

"Should you indeed?" Charlotte inquired. "I suppose Mr. Parker has puffed Sir Edward up into an object of fascination?"

"Oh, he told me a lot about him, he talked all through the

journey. I never knew a person could talk so much in a carriage. He has a very clever way of speaking above the clatter you know. But is he handsome, Charlotte, this infamous Edward Denham?"

"He is considered gloriously handsome by silly women and sensible ones alike. Handsome is a relative thing though, Abigail, a man's physical attributes are quickly rendered less becoming if his character is ugly and the reverse is often the case, a less well-favored man who has gentleman-like manners and earnest feelings will eventually outshine all dazzling rivals."

Abigail laughed. "Then I take it Sir Edward Denham, even in your eyes, is very, very handsome indeed, but I am obliged not to like him because you do not!"

"It is true, I do not like him. There you understand me perfectly. I confess he is a beautiful-looking sort of man but I should not care to look upon his elegance with regularity, there is almost certainly a high price to be paid for the privilege."

"Is he charming?" was Abigail's next question, and her sister answered with as much patience as could be roused in her, for she was convinced that Abigail would risk herself in liking such a man.

"He is an expert on captivation, the very embodiment of all that is charismatic. He is attentive, when he chooses to be, poetic, well-mannered, and accommodating. He is elegant in a contrived way. He wears the finest clothes. Feel free to faint away when you see him in his green coat, Abigail. He is something quite spectacular in the way of appearance and attractiveness. But all this derives from nothing more than learned skills and applied appeal, he has no genuine sentiment, women are mere instruments to him, he knows how to play them well enough but I fear the music will always be slightly off-key. I declare he believes himself capable of seducing any woman in the world."

"Your black-hearted account of Sir Edward does not correspond with Mr. Parker's description, Charlotte."

"I would not expect it to. Mr. Parker cares only for numbers. Sir Edward Denham is but one person amongst many who stay in

Sanditon, that is all the recommendation our host needs. Besides, Mr. Parker has not been subjected to Sir Edward Denham's wiles!"

"And you *have*?" cried Abigail with eagerness.

Charlotte scolded her sister. "Calm yourself, his attentions do nothing to make me unique, any woman, be she equipped with arms, legs, and a head is a likely victim. We are all, from the plainest to the fairest of us, subjected to his poetic ramblings at some point. They may set sillier hearts aflutter but they have little effect on me."

Abigail's fascination could not be concealed. "Oh my goodness, I do hope he picks on *me* next, I long to have a man recite poetry to me. Nothing ever happens in Willingden, I should be glad of the opportunity to enjoy a little flirtation. I do so adore the idea of a man who can recall poetry at whim. There is a dreaminess in it. I wish him to choose me."

"It is a harmless enough wish, Abigail, but I fear you will have to content yourself with someone other than Sir Edward Denham, he is to leave for London tomorrow morning. But do not be down-hearted, you may well be picked out for a florid farewell."

"You think I *will* meet him before he leaves then?"

"Depend upon it, Abigail, what little I know of Sir Edward leads me to say with absolute certainty that he will make a great performance of his departure. He will, you can be certain, overshadow Garrick, Kemble, and Kean."

CHAPTER 21

It was to Abigail's delight and Charlotte's chagrin that Sir Edward Denham called at Trafalgar House prior to his departure. He fawned enough over the younger Miss Heywood to satisfy her desire for flirtation; he was overt in his feigned admiration, expressive in his speech, and permanently poised on the edge of overfamiliarity. Abigail felt she would never be done with swooning but it was to Charlotte that Sir Edward directed his most poetic farewell.

"Ae fond kiss, and then we sever!" cried he, grasping Charlotte's hand amorously.

"A farewell and then forever!" retorted Charlotte, with a little too much emphasis on the "forever." While her misquoting of Burns might afford Sir Edward a small feeling of superiority, her adamant delivery made him quite uncomfortable.

"You disapprove of me, Miss Heywood," cried Sir Edward, his face the very picture of mortification, "that much is evident, but I shall continue to think fondly of you while you think ill of me."

As good an opportunity as this to put such a man to rights could not be squandered by Charlotte and she responded with more than a little relish. "I fear you misunderstand me, Sir. I certainly shall *not* think ill of you, indeed, I shall venture not to think of you at all." The curt manner of this farewell piqued Abigail's interest and after the gentleman had departed (he certainly felt his dejection more than he showed it), she made clear to her sister that she wished to pursue the matter that was intriguing her.

"Why so strong a disapproval, Charlotte? He is flirtatious to be sure, but can you not conceive that his behavior represents little more than an innocuous amusement? I confess to enjoying his attentions. We get nothing of the sort from the farm boys at home. He is sophisticated. He seemed a true gentleman to me."

"Abigail, please! You are too willing to approve of him, your youthful enthusiasm is admirable and refreshing, but that you want him to be good will not necessarily make him so. I understand your excitement, and when compared with farm boys, Sir Edward will appear noble. But you have not had the chance to observe his character, you cannot ascertain what he is."

"I know very well that the man is a compulsive tease, I do not need your powers of observation, or your seniority, to deduce that, but are you not a little hasty in making so harsh a judgment of him?"

"I assure you, Abigail, I am not. I had not been at Sanditon a week before I witnessed the severe effects of Sir Edward's artifice."

Abigail heard Charlotte's interpretation of how Clara Brereton came to be so indisposed with alarm. She was reticent to believe that Sir Edward Denham was entirely responsible for Miss Brereton's misfortune; furthermore, she was startled by her sister's readiness to accuse when the facts seemed so scant. Could he be wholly culpable? What had gone before? Charlotte was ever inclined to judge quickly, but to judge so wrongly? Abigail could only wonder. Her elder sister, whom she held in high esteem, had recently confessed that the effects of her propensity for rapid appraisal had resulted in tragic personal circumstances. If she could so misjudge a man who she loved, then heaven knew how ill-equipped she was to judge properly one she so disliked.

Viewed in a prejudiced light Sir Edward Denham would indeed be seen as little more than a philanderer, but, viewed with benevolence, he might appear no more villainous than any other young man with a penchant for female admiration. There was, Abigail thought, something healthful in his manner. Where Charlotte was quick-witted, fast to judge, and clever, Abigail was slow and less inclined to think ill of people than her sister was. Curiously disposed to frivolity, and yet not fickle, Abigail Heywood's propensity for fun was merely the product of her youth, her country upbringing, and an innate impulse to view life as a means of entertainment. When in Willingden she had begged to be allowed to go to Sanditon. Now there, she would certainly be eager to go to London, but until such time as *that* would be allowed she must content herself with Sanditon. There would be no lack of diversion, the Hollises had arrived, and the new surgeon and his nurse would follow.

"You will like my Dr. Wellscott, Mary," said Mr. Parker during dinner that evening. "He is as fine a fellow as could be found anywhere in the world and very eager to be settled here. His nurse, as we shall call her, is a very accommodating young woman, very accommodating indeed. I showed her my ankle you know and she had the presence of mind to suggest I keep clear of false calves! My goodness! I laughed at the idea but truly, my dear, was not that inspired? I am somewhat surprised that she took me as a man of fashion. I confess I never once thought of shaping my legs in my entire life but if ever I had, her advice would surely prove invaluable. Perhaps she meant to flatter me! To think of an old man like me padding my legs! But it says a lot for the place, do you not think, that she has the idea of us being such leaders, so à la mode. I daresay she has Sanditon in her mind as a fashionable spot like London. In any case, great improvements shall now take place here at our treasured little town. We already have the Hollises, that makes a total of five new faces to the town! Five!"

"Six, if you include me, I love Sanditon so much already I could stay forever," said Abigail.

"Of course!" cried Mr. Parker happily. "Pray do not feel yourself overlooked, child. I think it fair to say I see you so much as part of the family that I missed your head in the count. So there it is. Six new faces, we shall be bursting here at Sanditon, and what a happy overcrowding it shall be."

"Not *so* overcrowded, Sir, we already have the loss of Sir Edward to consider," said Charlotte solemnly, "and I am sure I am not the only one who believes that the absence of his vanity alone leaves a space large enough to fill with several more personalities."

Mr. Parker laughed. "Ah, you are a free spirit, Miss Charlotte, you speak as you find, it is no wonder my brother was so captivated by you." There was a silence at once uncomfortable and telling. Mr. Parker, seeing his error immediately, attempted to lessen the effect of his blunder, thereby attracting more attention to it and worsening the situation. "You and Sidney are both great wits, my dear. I am sure you will enjoy laughing together at some future date, for where there is no love lost there is always room for amusing reflection."

Charlotte remained quiet and, thinking Mr. Parker at his most ridiculous that afternoon, deigned to distract him. There was no difficulty found in trying to steer him from the subject of Sidney, one had only to mention some trifling aspect of Sanditon to be ensured of an overlong but enthusiastically given narrative. This she did and all the members of the party gained some small measure of satisfaction from being afforded the opportunity to eat and drink and listen without a single one of them being troubled to say anything at all.

Had he been merely a new visitor to Sanditon Dr. Wellscott could have relied on an exuberant welcome, but the rather embarrassing truth was that his status as surgeon afforded him a reception the grandeur of which would not have seemed out of place had it been designed for a monarch. It was decided by Mr. Parker, with his long suffering wife's approval, that Dr. Wellscott must be very properly received; a formal invitation to Trafalgar House would afford the good doctor the opportunity to meet a small selection of those who were soon to become his patients, and, likewise gain introductions to those who were not. Mrs. Parker heard her husband with trepidation.

"Pray do not consider another garden party." Her quiet tone displayed nothing of the violent reservations she was harboring. "It is all too soon, Tom. Why, the lawns have scarce recovered from the last one. I noticed some fashionables wore those dreadful high red heels. The grass is quite spiked through since. The gardener cannot put me at ease on this point with his talk of aerating the earth. I think we may have over-ventilated our garden. The grass is simply punctured, a muddied mess of holes and unsightly divots."

"No, no, Mary! A garden party will not do in any case," said Mr. Parker with no reference to or sympathy for his wife's concerns for the lushness of the green. "I have in mind a smaller, more select guest list for an *indoor* assembly, a supper or dinner party would do very well, and I think it prudent to invite those persons who are most likely to consider themselves in need of medicine in the future by way of promoting the doctor."

Charlotte could not remain silent. "On that premise, Mr. Parker, you shall surely end with the sickliest of company!"

"My dear, Miss Heywood, I do not expect *all* of Dr. Wellscott's patients to be unwell!"

"In all honesty *I* do not expect any of them to be unwell. For what ailment can thrive in such a sanatorium as Sanditon?"

Mr. Parker exclaimed, "My dear girl, you have quite my way of thinking on the matter, I'll wager the majority who seek Dr. Wellscott's prescriptions will be as sound in body as you or I but, if their purses allow it, they will seek his advice just the same. It is simply the way of things, a good doctor we have needed and a good doctor we now shall have, the effects will be far reaching, Miss Heywood, the incapacitated shall flee from Bath to Sanditon as soon as news reaches there."

The Miss Beauforts and Mrs. Griffiths were included on the guest list.

"They travel about, you know, that is as good an advertisement for our town as any, it would be improvident to overlook them. Alas! Miss Lambe is already gone away, but there is a girl who would sincerely benefit from Dr. Wellscott's expertise. And I sorely miss her presence her for there is something exotic in her looks that adds appeal to the place. The English thrill to meet foreigners, especially in their own country," said Mr. Parker.

Lady Denham was judged too unwell to accept an invitation but, considering it remiss to exclude her, Mr. Parker issued one in the full expectation of its being declined. "I shall compensate accordingly, I do believe she would be most grateful if Dr. Wellscott were to go to Sanditon House and visit her personally."

"How can you be sure of Lady Denham's welcoming your doctor, Sir? Does not she blame a physician for her husband's death? I am sure she attributes her general good health to the avoidance of all remedies but the salt water, the sea air, her milch asses, and Mr. Hollis's chamber-horse," said Charlotte.

"I do not think Lady Denham has ever used the chamber-horse, Charlotte," cried Mr. Parker. "And as for her remonstrances about the medical profession, well, those were merely the sentiments of the robust! And long-forgotten, I daresay. Lady Denham has since fallen victim to illness. Her milch asses may have served her well when she was in good health. Likewise the sea air; everyone knows I can always account for the good of the sea air *and* salt water, but I am now persuaded," this with a knowing look at his wife, "that my good doctor will be graciously received and welcomed at Sanditon House. In confidence, I am inclined to believe that Lady Denham resented the ten fees the old doctor charged to attend her husband. My Dr. Wellscott is different, he has something of fairness in him I am sure."

"In fairness then," said Charlotte with a wry smile, "let us agree that the payment of ten fees, for the service of killing one man, once, does seem excessive."

CHAPTER 22

The dinner provided in honor of the surgeon's newly taken residency at Sanditon was arranged with all the expediency of an emergency and all the reverence that might usually be reserved for the nobility. Lists were drawn up, menus discussed with the housekeeper and cook and, although it pained Mr. Parker to admit it, it was agreed that some supplies must be ordered from London. There were heated arguments over the removables and the corner dishes, and an attack of hysteria, on the part of the cook, at the suggestion of buttered lobster and several French dishes. Each detail of the arrangements might have been more carefully considered had Mr. Parker not been so infused with urgency. On his wife's inquiring about the necessity of a fancy centerpiece he said, "Nothing too large nor too small, my dear, something elegant but not overpowering, something representative of our good town. Something appropriate for a surgeon."

Charlotte, whose reluctance to become wrapped up in the proceedings counted for very little, cried, "Perhaps an apothecary's jar in place of a vase or if you sincerely mean to follow the theme, bandaging might do as well as any cloth for the table. So well indeed, it would be a pity to remove it at dessert." At this, Mrs. Parker frowned but her husband smiled knowingly.

"Your high spirits are promotion indeed for Sanditon, Miss Heywood," declared the latter, "how much you find to laugh about, how truly happy your disposition, how essentially humorous your character has become. It is hard not to smile by the sea, is it not, Miss Heywood?"

Not wishing to deny Mr. Parker the pleasure of believing that location rather than disposition was the cause of her good humor,

Charlotte responded quietly, "With all my heart, Sir, I am sure I could never smile so easily in another place."

Mr. Parker, so delighted with the world in general, and particularly pleased with Charlotte, proclaimed life a thorough success and announced that he would not be opposed to spending several pounds more than budgeted on the proposed evening's entertainment. Mrs. Parker felt the expenditure and excitement to be unwarranted but she was put firmly in her place by her husband.

"Mary! While it pains me to cause you any worry, I must remind you that Morgan is quite equal to the task and our cook's instructions, if you have any concern over them, will be quite simple. We may not boast the advantage of a French chef but Heavens above, my dear, I am not so foolish as to be planning one hundred and twelve dishes!" Mr. Parker's mind was soon on dessert. "Upon my word, I do so hanker after a forcing garden; it is the very thing to serve exotic fruits these days. Some have it that too much fruit excites the stomach but I never had a moment's anxiety with fruit of any sort, cooked or fresh. No, indeed, I would honestly welcome a pineapple or two. Nevertheless, we shall do with what they have at Sanditon House. Andrew, the gardener there, stays with what he knows but serves us well enough. We may not have glamour in our puddings but the regular summer fruits are not to be frowned upon." On the subject of expense, he said nothing more than, "Pray, spare us all the vulgarity of counting coins, Mary."

Invitations were sent, received, and returned. The party was to consist of Mr. and Mrs. Parker, Charlotte, Abigail, Diana, Susan, and Arthur, Mrs. Griffiths, the Miss Beauforts, the three Hollises, and several Sanditonians who had been deemed suitable either by the nature and severity of their ailments or the size of their purses. The guests of honor were, naturally, Dr. Wellscott and his nurse. It was decided, with Lady Denham unable to attend, that Dr. Wellscott himself would lead the party in to dinner. With numbers totaling five and twenty it was agreed that there was a very high risk that the good doctor, such was his novelty, might be swamped. Every attempt, Mr. Parker insisted, to relieve the man of unnecessary suffocation was to be made.

"We must avoid situations that might force the poor fellow to talk business all of the evening, much as I am eager to promote him I fear too zealous an approach might overwhelm him."

"And medicinal matters are not generally considered appropriate subjects for discussion at dinner," observed Charlotte. "There is a very real danger of appetites being lost I think."

"Quite so! You have it exactly right. Restraint must be encouraged. If any amongst the party wish to seek Dr. Wellscott's advice, they should be urged to do so, but not publicly, not socially," said Mr. Parker.

"Indeed not," said Charlotte. "Let them save their ill heads and fevers for other more seemly occasions."

"Occasions that must be paid for, Miss Heywood, not to be too harsh upon our residents, but some people are notoriously adept at wheedling advice when they might otherwise be expected to pay for it. Such is the medical man's lot, I gather. Preposterous really, one would not expect a tailor to hand out new breeches to everyone he happened to meet at a gathering, but doctors are, I am sorry to say, oft victims of a certain type of robbery and I want none of it for my dear Wellscott."

CHAPTER 23

Wellscott was a man whose five and forty years had served him well, he was too broadly built to be considered elegant, but his features were good and strong, his eyes the very representation of kindness, and his curls would have been admired had they been less unruly. He had gone about the world in a state of utter dedication, devoted as he was to his chosen profession, but it could not honestly be said that he excelled in his medical endeavors. His knowledge and his judgment were sound enough, but without that sturdiness of mind that other men of his profession possessed, he was inclined to allow the healthy to believe themselves ailing, if they wished it, and agreed, rather too readily, to oblige their whims. Moreover, he had a propensity to provide potions and pills for anyone who took a fancy to having them. Having made neither a serious diagnosis nor a serious mistake during his twenty years in practice, he had maintained his position creditably and now, in his forty-sixth year, was congratulating himself on having fallen into such a fortuitous situation as was to be his at Sanditon.

The only blemish that sullied his rosy view of life was his bachelor state. A good wife, he had lately thought, would prove an asset, a companion, and he had quietly convinced himself that at least one of the ladies, those expected to descend in their multitudes to his little seaside practice, would possess all the irresistible attributes that would induce him to make a proposal. He harbored few fixed ideas about what such a woman would be like, had made no general observations of other ladies in his acquaintance to have any notion of what pleased him and what did not. He was fond enough of dark eyes but not so smitten by them as to lessen the chances of a blue-eyed lady. He had but one prerequisite, one single aspect that was, to him, essential. The lady, whoever she might be and wherever she might come from, must love a book as ardently as he did. She must be a devourer of words, a lover of stories, a woman, not too highly academic as to induce terror in her husband, but a person improved enough to be equal to enjoying a book and perhaps later discussing it.

Dr. Wellscott's books, though too few to constitute claims to the collection being a library, were his most valued possessions. Though it was only nominally impressive, he prized his small selection of volumes above any other material thing. He was heartened to find therefore, on appraising the small drawing room that was newly his own at the house he was to occupy at Sanditon, that one alcove to the right of the chimney breast housed a handsome breakfront bookcase which seemed designed exactly, by way of its capacity, to hold his own most treasured publications.

Charlotte's immediate liking for both Dr. Wellscott and his nurse allowed a momentary warmth to settle in her troubled heart. Wellscott, amongst the eager party of guests, conducted himself with affability and Maisie, although of a timid appearance, impressed Charlotte by giving the impression of there being more to her spirit, her character, and her history than could ever be revealed during so brief an acquaintance. She was a small, pink-faced young woman, with more of the girl about her than her age might otherwise have dictated. It was thought she was around four and twenty, but there was to be no more clarity on the subject than that. She was a watchful creature, her dark eyes seemed always to be darting around the room, they sparkled when a joke was told and were the very illustration of sympathy when tales of woe were recounted. "I have ne'er seen such eyes as hers," thought Charlotte. "They are so apparently open, so easily they convey sincerity, yet … am I deceived by her? Could such eyes delude me? I fear they could, but hope they do not, for I like her; I like her very well, indeed."

Oh, dear Charlotte Heywood. Would not you think, reader, that her tendency to evaluate people and circumstances with no foundation to do so might now have been abated by her mistaken assessment of Sidney Parker? Would not you have hoped that a lesson needing desperately to be learned had now been learned? But Charlotte, whose faults were no more evil than are characteristic of a good deal of humans, was not ready to reform yet, she was cut out for quick judgment, overanalysis, and ill-formed conclusions. The peculiarity lies in the fact that, although she was often wrong, there were occasions when she was not. But to speak so is to condemn poor Maisie, to presume, Heywood style, that the girl was a keeper of secrets. And so, for the sake of judging steadily, we must be resigned to form our own opinions, to allow time to offer us all the facts.

There was certainly a look about Maisie that one would not expect to see in a person who lacked the advantage of education, there was in her eyes a substantial degree of intelligent scrutiny, a bright intensity it might be called. Recognition showed in them when various matters, which were thought to be beyond her comprehension, were raised. On these subjects she never commented, while her eyes proved her understanding, her words were not about to reveal it. She remained quiet, speaking only when prompted and while the world about her talked incessantly, on this matter or that, she merely smiled. She could not be described as beautiful. But it can justly be said that the criteria for such an accolade is generally so obscure and so prone to rapid change as to make it almost an impossibility for any woman to lay claim to it with any assurance of its being permanent. Even those who are judged fair often struggle to live up to the honor.

Maisie's features were pleasing although not fine, her hair, her complexion both tolerably good by way of her youth and her demeanour and manners were by no means lacking. Yet, despite all that was in her favor, there seemed an air of deficiency about her, a difficulty in expressing herself that Charlotte, at least, felt compelled to appease. "If she would only speak a little more, I am convinced I should find her amiable and equally persuaded that for her own comfort it would be beneficial to make at least one friend," thought she.

CHAPTER 24

Dinners held in honor of one particular guest put a very definite stress upon the recipient, lucky though they may feel themselves in being so singled out, there can be nothing worse than sensing that expectations must be lived up to. Dr. Wellscott was no exhibitionist, and fortuitous this was indeed, for Mr. Parker, secure, elevated, and puffed up out of all reasonable proportion, was always ready to display himself and his beloved Sanditon to best advantage when in the comfort of his own home. A brief speech was all that was demanded of the good doctor.

"Nothing lengthy, my dear fellow, no need to talk yourself hoarse, but I do feel our party would appreciate it. You are an important addition to our town, Sir, unceremonious though we are here, there are some formalities worth adhering to, they pay dividends," said Mr. Parker. And so it was that Dr. Wellscott, quite perplexed by the prominence his arrival seemed to be acquiring, prepared a written guideline for himself in order that his address might be delivered with apparent ease.

The assembly went off well. Wellscott talked, smiled, nodded, and enthused tirelessly. He spoke charmingly to all the ladies present and found himself, by the end of the evening, to be quite the favorite. By the end of his first week, he had been entirely swamped by Sanditon's headaches, ill humors, backaches, and sprains. Illness, imagined or actual, found its way to his door, he soothed febrile brows and troubled minds, gave out pastes and pills, and no less than sixteen bottles of linctus in one afternoon alone. Mr. Parker, as soon he had the chance to inquire as to the doctor's progress, was eager to be the first to hear the report.

"It was a very good week's work, Tom, and only the one fever case needing the blood let out and that was Mrs. Leatham who fancies herself melancholy one day and choleric the next. I am no eager phlebotomist, Mr. Parker, but what must be done must be done and the lady, I am glad to say, felt the benefits immediately. She has inordinately obliging skin, very *pale* skin, and the veins are the easiest in the world to locate. Oh! I see you squirm, Mr. Parker, forgive me, I forget myself with matters of the body. I comprehend your aversion, I really do. The finer points of my profession used to affect me in the same way, I am more accustomed to the functions of human beings now but as I say, I do not let the blood without regretting the need to. Thankfully I am not often obliged to pick up a lancet or a fleam!" said Dr. Wellscott.

"The tools of your trade quite confound me," said Mr. Parker, clearly shaken, "but I daresay you have the measure of them all."

"For the most part, my dear man, I find instruments alarming. The brutality of them always impresses me greatly. Nevertheless, we doctors are lured into liking our implements by way of their being so well-crafted. There is much to recommend an ebony-handled scalpel so long as one does not too long consider its impact on the flesh."

"Ah, on the subject of apparatus, did I ever mention that Lady Denham keeps a chamber-horse? It belonged to her first husband, Mr. Hollis. I cannot vouch for *its* being well-crafted, I do not think I ever saw the thing, but I hear of it from time to time and understand that it could be had on reasonable terms. I can report nothing of its benefits. It did not do the owner much good, Sir, he is dead."

"Sir, I do not recollect any mention of a chamber-horse, but let us fix it that I shall not advocate the use of one. A chair on boards can never imitate a first-rate animal. The very thought of indoor riding seems to me ridiculous. One must be starved of air. I never knew a good man mount a chamber-horse in all my days."

"Might not some of the ladies prefer the solitude and privacy of the indoors though, Sir?"

"If they intend to forgo dignity and ride without being obliged to sit to the side, then I daresay the confines of four walls and drawn blinds would be considered a blessing."

"Surely, Sir, no lady deserves the title who would abandon her dignity in such a manner, privately or otherwise."

"You understand then my failure to see any benefit in those machines. What has such a contraption to offer that a good brisk walk and fresh air cannot provide?"

Mr. Parker nodded solemnly. "I am entirely in agreement with you, Dr. Wellscott, entirely."

Enamored were the sick, intrigued were the healthy and Dr. Wellscott, by the beginning of his second week in practice, rejoiced in the glow that a flourishing new business must always excite. Almost immediately Maisie found her duties increased. She mixed liquids, ground powders, steeped bandages, and took samples. In addition, she visited. The feeble and the hardy all clamored to have Dr. Wellscott's good nurse attend them and the sight of her purposefully scurrying form dashing from one house to another during the day became so regular and accepted that very soon it was hard to imagine that she had not always been there.

Sanditon, you see, was an embracing town, a place with an affectionate grasp, an allure, an indescribable means of capturing the spirit. To its salty bosom, even the coolest heart could not help but be enfolded. Its very air and sounds mesmerized. Gulls screeched overhead, sea spray spattered the buildings leaving rusty tears trickling from windows. Waves crashed or gently rolled and fishing boats slept on the shore. It was beguiling and was set to become more so now that it could boast expertise in the area of medicine.

Lady Denham, still indisposed, was eager to see the doctor so long as fees could be kept "reasonable." Moreover, she was gladdened by the prospect of having weekly visits from his nurse. "She will be a great comfort, and should she feel inclined I daresay she might read to me," said Lady Denham to the doctor.

"Ah, my dear Lady Denham," cried he, "my nurse does not read. I hope this will not disappoint you."

Resigned, but not discouraged, Lady Denham said, "Then I shall read to *her*, when it suits me, and there is our solution! Send the girl on Wednesdays! Pray warn her of my state, the old can shock the young. Decay is wholly unattractive. Youthful eyes oft see their own mortality when they witness it in others. Vanity I am beyond, but insensible I am not, I would not wish to alarm." All this from a woman who, to the good doctor, seemed hearty enough for her seventy-odd years. Her eyes were as bright as could be expected and when she wished some book or object to be nearer to her she removed swiftly from her chair and got herself about the room in order to retrieve it with more than a little spring in her step.

Chapter 25

Habits, good and bad, are formed quickly. Routines and regimes are decided upon and enforced with startling rapidity. Wednesday, habit now had it, was to be Maisie's day for visiting Lady Denham. Thursdays would see her attending Mrs. Griffiths who, despite never having suffered a day's serious illness in her life, found that her spirits were somewhat depleted by Miss Lambe's absence. The Miss Beauforts provided little comfort there; each was so wrapped up in the other that they paid scant attention to their guardian. And so, for the most part, Mrs. Griffiths contented herself with the letters she received from Miss Lambe.

For two days in a row Maisie was to be read to; Wednesdays were devoted to the poetic; the odes of Collins, tales from Crabbe, and Cowper's "The Castaway" were all read with feeling and listened to with fervor, but on Thursdays, how different a style of story she would hear. Miss Lambe's letters intrigued her and she felt, by way of Mrs. Griffiths's tireless description of their writer, that she knew young Miss Lambe as well as any person she had actually met. Eastbourne! What a haven it sounded. Miss Lambe was having treatment there but it was mentioned by Mrs. Griffiths that a lot of inconvenience might have been avoided had Dr. Wellscott been brought to Sanditon sooner. "Then my dear Miss Lambe would have been able to stay here, but," said she with a smile both knowing and secretive, "if she had, then a certain event, a certain rather pleasing development might never have taken place." Imprudent though it might have been for Mrs. Griffiths to speak so of her charge's personal life, Maisie relished every detail.

"It is a funny thing, is it not, Miss Maisie, that they were both here in Sanditon without so much of a hint of regard apparent, yet removed to Eastbourne a romance begins to flourish between them! He has family in Sanditon so I expect, should the attachment continue to a desirous end, that the wedding would take place here."

What joy Thursdays were! They could not be hurried to come soon enough and Maisie was grateful that one of the Parker boys had fallen from a gatepost and quite badly hurt an elbow, a knee, and a forehead. In attending the poor child, she found her mind was quite occupied and for as many days as could be managed in the week, she was called upon to attend him. He was an innately good child, better now for the restraint that his injuries put upon him. Each day she visited had the same pattern; he would chatter (his mind was lively), ask her to sing songs, play games, and do tricks, until exactly one hour later when he had quite worn himself out he would sleep, his little golden head angelically poised on his pillow for two hours at least. But Maisie was not to move, not to leave him, she must sit by him even when he slumbered with as much vigilance as was expected from her when he was awake.

Now, could she have picked up a book to amuse herself then an hour or two of sitting might have been made more acceptable. To have some amusement, some occupation, would at least have made two long hours seem like one short one. As she could not turn to a book for comfort, she greatly appreciated Charlotte's visiting her and the friendship, which the latter had thought the former so in need of, thus developed. Charlotte was at odds, Abigail was no companion, she had lately taken to visiting Diana, Susan, and Arthur and was rarely to be found at Trafalgar House and so talking with Maisie fast became a pastime that Charlotte looked forward to. Gossiping is, for the most part, viewed as an undignified mode of entertainment; nevertheless, it is also one of the most enjoyable. Maisie, no talebearer by nature, soon found herself animated in Charlotte's company; she was encouraged by her companion's enthusiasm to talk and talk and talk. But with what could she regale her friend other than news handed down? Their minds were soon in Eastbourne and all the details of Mrs. Griffiths's letters from

Miss Lambe were recounted.

"It is thought that Miss Lambe," said Maisie quietly, "will marry soon, you must know the gentleman, Charlotte, he went to Eastbourne from here, Mrs. Griffiths says he has family here in Sanditon." Charlotte, now paralyzed with horror, wished tears could flow but knew they must not. Sidney! It was as she had feared and suspected. Sidney, his affections rebounding, had fallen in love with Miss Lambe. Oh to bear it was impossible, to think of him now more painful than ever it had been. She had hoped at least that his misery might have continued for a while longer. Was not so rapid a recovery to be felt as an insult? So, he had forgotten her, abandoned all feelings for her, he was cured and with a heart freshly healed was obviously more than inclined to love another. "I am all misery," thought she. "All hope is gone. I cannot hear this. I cannot think of him."

Maisie, not entirely insensible to Charlotte's sudden pallor, was querulous but her charge's golden head stirred on the pillow, and on waking he demanded drinks, games, and attention and so the two suddenly-hushed gossipers were then engaged in his entertainment and his entertainment alone. Charlotte, powerfully aware of the perils of idle talk, pleaded a headache and sought respite in her room. With a heart restless and broken she cried herself to sleep, even then, she could not escape her sorrows, she dreamed of weddings, of happy scenes and in all of these she was but a spectator. She was nothing more than a passerby witnessing the euphoria of others with a spirit fragmented and shattered.

CHAPTER 26

Surprises always bring about a freshness to a scene and Arthur Parker's proposal of marriage to Abigail Heywood was a surprise indeed. Theirs had been a rapid love affair, born of a mutual liking, and a shared desire on the part of each to escape the confines that their respective families had imposed upon them. They were not ill-suited, neither was their love violent, but there was regard enough for the basis of a successful marriage. It is so hard to be happy on behalf of others when one's own spirit is heavy with personal woe but Charlotte smiled and congratulated and enthused over her sister's good fortune as best she could. Her own heart, of course, broke a little more as she did so. Abigail's head was full of flowers, gowns, and wedding breakfasts; she was to be married from Sanditon.

"But our mother and father," Charlotte warned, "have not left Willingden over a handful of times in their entire lives!"

Abigail was merriment itself. "They will be persuaded to come for such a happy event," she cried.

Maisie, so newly acquainted with Sanditon, was thrilled to have such news so soon. Weddings are great uniters as well as great dividers. Conversation on Thursdays quite revolved around the Parker-Heywood union and on one Thursday in particular, Mrs. Griffiths was found not reading a letter, as was usual, but composing one.

"I am writing to our dear Miss Lambe, Maisie," she said, gesturing for the girl to sit by her, "but I fear I must keep this missive short. The doctor will have told you I have sprained my wrist. Do you see?" she said, displaying her forearm. "I was helping Miss

Beaufort to tune her harp, wretched article, when my hand quite seized. I daresay the garden party weakened it to start with. One is always obliged to hold up one's skirts to walk on grass. We ladies suffer the most intricate injuries. Dr. Wellscott has sent the poultice, I hope."

"Yes, ma'am," Maisie replied.

"Well, I shall finish my letter, though Heaven's above, the Lord knows it is a struggle to do so, but finish I must, then you may see to my wrist. I have so much to tell Miss Lambe, I truly regret writing in this scant manner for I know she relishes a nice long read. However, I keep only to the major points you see and find I can fit quite a history onto one side alone." She spoke while writing and was coming to the point of applying her signature and her regards when she threw up her hands. "What am I about, Miss Maisie? I clean forgot to mention that Miss Abigail is betrothed to Arthur Parker! Oh dear me, I shall include that as a postscript, there, it will fit just neatly here if I restrict myself to the bare particulars."

So, with wrist swollen and no more space on the bottom of the page than would hold a "God Bless You" she wrote: *Recently engaged, Miss Heywood-Mr. Parker.* "Pounce the page for me, Maisie," she said. "My injury prevents me, I never have held with blotting, it weakens the ink." Duly the girl powdered the letter and that afternoon when gossip was over, bandages applied, and letters gone to the post, Mrs. Griffiths declared that it would be beneficial all round if Maisie were to improve herself and obtain the skill of reading and writing. And, although it meant she had to stay an hour later than usual, she began, under Mrs. Griffiths's instruction to absorb the basics of the alphabet, learning so quickly that by the time she left her tutor was inspired to say, "Never have I known a person acquire any skill so fast."

The Miss Beauforts, somewhat disconcerted that full-blown romance had not come their way, had taken solace in the company of the Hollises. In Eliza and Julia they found they had fair companions and in William Hollis they were gratified to discover that they had what they sought most, an admirer. Their charms were not lost to him, and although none of the three thought their association would ever mean more than just a mild flirtation, the trio was satisfied enough with that and very soon the sight of the triad parading the promenade or frequenting the library was commonplace. It is always greatly satisfying when flirtatious young women find a devotee; they can then be happily occupied, hour after hour, by his attentions. They live to be in his gaze and flounder when they are not, whether they think anything of him at all is not to be guessed at, it is merely his sex and his flattery they seek and thrive on. Had not William Hollis elected to play this role it is without doubt the Miss Beauforts would have had no trouble in securing the regard of another, they excelled in temptation, and although they had thus far failed with Sir Edward, their eager praise-seeking spirits were not to be dampened.

Sanditon summers, although not longer than summers elsewhere, seemed extended, felt warmer, and had a sense of endlessness about them. The sight of sun on sea is one that is always promising and that year, with all that was going on in Sanditon, it seemed that the promotion so wished for by Mr. Parker was a certainty. Wellscott had never known such business; Maisie was learning to read; a wedding was planned; and sales at Jebbs and the library had seen an increase, which could only be accounted for, according to Mr. Parker, by the general atmosphere of happiness and prosperity that surrounded the place. Was Charlotte's the only case of despondence? To her it felt likely that all around her were in a kind of ecstasy, a delighted contentment. "Such joy eludes me," thought she, "and, so long as I allow my heart to be owned outright by one who has no wish to cherish it, it always shall. I must quell my anguish as he has done. I must, with effort that seems beyond me, endeavor to heal, to restore."

A fortnight was not time enough to cure Charlotte entirely, but it was time enough to allow her to give in to a reluctant acceptance that if Sidney did not love her anymore then she must not think of him further. With her feelings thus harnessed, she went about, half sad and half resigned, yet to her this was almost a state of contentment. Her impassioned tears had all been cried, her anger spent. Her love (at least she had been honest enough to own it to herself) was not to be stifled, it lived in her, warm and painful (in a sense neither dull nor piercing but constant) and so much a part of her now as to be accepted as a general feeling. She was damped down, diluted in spirit, a half functioning version of her previous self, but she was surviving. She could smile more readily in company, would play the pianoforte as best she could, but not sing, for the entertainment of others and took part, in as full a way as could be expected of her, in the daily and nightly situations that made up Sanditon life.

There came a point, around the time that the Parker boy was recovered, that she even considered herself mended. Maisie's visits would now halt, which was a matter of regret to both and Charlotte's initial idea was for the two to continue their meetings, but in this she was to have no success, so sought after was a visit from Dr. Wellscott's nurse, that there was no longer a day in the week that found Maisie free. She was snatched up by other residents as soon her availability was made known, and a good deal of money was put her way in lieu of her attentions.

Charlotte could not help but think of Sidney. So there was a vow quickly broken. She could sometimes recall his features with accuracy and at other times, she could not conjure his face at all. She might hear a snippet of conversation in her mind and have his voice clear as life resounding in her ears for some time after. She would see a figure strolling the street or descending from a carriage and fleetingly imagine it to be him. The imagination of the heartbroken is torturous indeed. All these symptoms of adoration our Charlotte displayed, but determination made her disregard them, like the dull pain that resided in her bosom, the products of her imagination became an accepted element of her being. She would see Sidney walking the park, or leaving the library, or coming up the path at Trafalgar House, but she only had to blink her eyes to banish him and something like calm acceptance would be restored in her heart.

Chapter 27

Abigail Heywood and Arthur Parker, so much the picture of youthful levity, were often to be found at Trafalgar House. They made such a sweet couple that no one could feel threatened by them or envious of them; nor could anyone, the Miss Beauforts being the exception, attribute the lovers' dedication to anything other than the most genuine of uncomplicated feelings. Abigail had had her moment of dreamy impracticality; she had swooned over Sir Edward Denham, savored meeting him, and secretly dreamed of securing such a man for herself.

But Abigail knew that dreams were for sleepers and reality for those who must keep awake in life and an Arthur Parker had been a catch so much more within her means than an Edward Denham would ever have been. Her practical sensibilities were entirely satisfied and her romantic needs more than catered for by Arthur's constant gazing at her as if he could scarce believe his luck. It was something, Abigail quickly realized, to be loved more than one loved, and the outcome was that she thought herself very lovely and very desirable to be able to inspire such devotion.

But love must not be allowed to overwhelm people and wedding arrangements must be made in all seriousness; even where the bride and her needs are modest, endless talk and plans (far more than is ever truly necessary) must abound. How wearisome the subject of dresses to a prospective husband! How mystifying such a man must find his future wife's propensity to discuss, for weeks on end, and without any sign of growing tired of the topic, the style of a gown that will be worn just once before being altered.

Arthur Parker, although very taken up with his *own* way of being in love, was by no means a fashionable man. He knew little of ceremonious affairs, cared nothing for them, and talk of the wedding arrangements simply washed over him.

One afternoon his beloved, in a state of unreasonable excitement, said, "The length of the sleeves and the style of the bouquet have everything to recommend them, but I fear such foliage will obscure the work on the bodice. That would be dreadful! I would not wish to have the best part of my dress concealed. It would upset the seamstress and mortify me. It is the only time I shall ever wear such a dress and I want it admired." At this Arthur merely nodded and smiled and, unable to comprehend the application of so much energy to so simple a thing as a choice of dress or the style of bouquet, settled upon walking in the garden. The air would clear his head, what good was it for him to have thoughts of muslins and ribbons thrust upon him? He was a man. Talk of pretty things was, in his view, entirely pointless.

Trafalgar House in the summer boasted a beautiful garden, even so late in the season with autumn threatening to burn the green from the leaves. The new plants were beginning to look established and, despite the gardens being more a plan than an accomplishment, there was something promising to be found there. Arthur, the fresh air being just the means to wipe his mind free of his loved one's trousseau, was musing to himself that his attachment to Abigail had brought a significant reduction in his bilious attacks. His health, in general, had improved. He thought, with more than a little smugness, of the future fulfillments and comforts that were now secured as his own. How true it must be that Sanditon was a restorative place.

"For I am cured!" he said aloud, "and happy and … " it seemed incredible but he went on to confess joyfully, " … in *love*?" He was as near to elation as he had ever been and, therefore, little prepared for any form of confrontation. But suffer such an encounter he must, for soon an adversary would be upon him, questioning, demanding, and accusing in a manner so violent and terrifying as to abolish all Arthur's previous feelings of gratification. Poor Arthur.

Sidney Parker was, and always had been, a good deal taller and stronger than his brother Arthur. The latter's first thoughts on seeing his elder brother were only of gladness. He, Arthur, concerned himself, upon regarding Sidney's determined approach toward him in the garden, with how elated a welcome he would show him. There was so much good news to impart! Alas, the friendly nature of Arthur's salutations was only to be disregarded and Sidney, with a look both grieved and angry in his eye, raised his voice to his brother.

"Arthur, I will not prevail upon you any longer than is necessary, for fear it might do damage to us both. You cannot think me arrived here for nothing. I have news of your engagement and wish only to know one thing." He was overwrought, distracted, and there was a very great need to steady himself before he posed the question which he could barely ask without a good deal of incredulity in his voice. "Do you *love* her?"

Was this some aggressive form of brotherly concern? Was it mere impudence? Or was it derangement? Surely Sidney could have no objection to his, Arthur's, intention to marry Abigail. Arthur was not the cleverest of men but he knew himself to be fortunate in securing Abigail's heart as his own. His brother, indeed his whole family, must surely share his relief at the success of his attachment. It had after all, been wholly unexpected that he, Arthur, would ever marry. That he, of all people, should have succeeded in gaining any woman's regard was a matter that could only be considered pleasing. His brother Sidney's apparent outrage did not make any sense at all.

Arthur recoiled from the impassioned questioning and answered quietly, with careful consideration of Sidney's agitated performance. "No less than I ought," said he, "and no more than is wise. I love in my own way," he said apologetically, "which is, I daresay, to be viewed as deficient in the eyes of those more prone to fervor, but the object of my affections does not complain, she does not find herself deprived, so I go along and go about as I see fit."

Sidney paled. "*And this*," cried he, all pain and astonishment, "is love enough for you I imagine, but is it really love enough for her?

I cannot believe your style, your relaxed manner, could truly satisfy her. I think you are very much deceived in her." He threw his coat off and cried in a mocking tone, "*She* does not complain! Ha! *She* does not find herself deprived! No! She clearly has an easy way of settling then, a very rapid manner of attaching and detaching wheresoever she pleases." He gave Arthur a look that indicated he demanded an explanation before he set off to walk in the garden.

The latter angered, he was not formed for passion; but he felt it now, all his placidity was gone in a moment. It was a new, unnerving experience and he felt the sensation worth savoring. It had so little ill-effect on his frailty and put such an incredible feeling of powerful determination in his heart that he was not about to forego the pleasure of the pain too swiftly. He was silent, on the point of being overrun by his sentiments when a rational thought occurred. "Sidney cannot be made sense of, he rants and cries about Abigail, but I cannot for the life of me recall hearing that he has ever met her," he thought. He smiled to himself. "I might be thought foolish," he said aloud, "but I am convinced there can only be a misunderstanding at the root of this outburst."

Arthur was quickly by Sidney, anxiety made the latter breathe heavily; minor exertion was the cause of the former's panting.

"What business is it of yours, brother, to show concern for a woman you do not know?" Arthur demanded.

"You describe her as a woman I do not know!" cried Sidney. "Why you are mistaken! I know her very well indeed and am convinced, though you may never comprehend the torment it causes me to say this, that *I* love her more than you ever could." He was quiet for a moment. "And yet I love her only as she deserves, with a heart fully anchored by intensity, with a soul that perishes without hers, with eyes that are blind to all but the sight of her, with appetite, longing, admiration, and agony combined is how I love her." These last three words were spoken with painful emphasis and the speaker, all his energy spent on saying them, seemed at once to lose height, weight, and composure.

Arthur put his hand to his weary brother's shoulder and said, with a wisdom beyond that expected of him, "But brother, you have not yet met Abigail."

There was something satisfying, Arthur felt, in clearing the matter up. So long had he felt himself inadequate to his sisters and both of his brothers. Now, with the prospect of his marriage, and the seriousness of matrimony and the life of a husband ahead of him, he felt himself superior, advanced. It was the first time he had ever experienced the delight of greater knowledge but he knew it to be something worth relishing.

There must have been tears, for men (particularly those of a feeling nature like Sidney Parker) will be obliged to cry at some point in their lives, and what better reason had Sidney, that afternoon, to shed tears than in relief? What joy he felt on knowing his dear Charlotte to be unattached, what utter completeness and hope claimed him. With resolve he sought her, to be given another chance to declare himself in her power was bliss indeed, to be on the threshold of seeing her again renewed him, charged him, and made his stride and his intentions both purposeful and true.

Mrs. Griffiths's letter had been the sole cause of Sidney's distress, it was her report alone that had persuaded him that his brother Arthur had set his sights on Charlotte. The relief he felt at finding himself mistaken was immeasurable.

CHAPTER 28

Sidney stood before Charlotte, yielding, willing her to want him, while she (had he but known it) wished nothing but to have him gone. She had failed to remove him with a blink of her eye for he was *really* there before her, talking, but she could not listen attentively. He spoke of marriage. "Oh! Pain of pains! Why does he come here to tell me of his own happiness? He cannot know I love him. There I must blame myself. Why should he think I feel anything other than contempt? Have I ever revealed my preference? He must think me impartial, he must see me as capable of delighting in Miss Lambe's good fortune!"

How many minutes passed Charlotte did not know, and many years later when it was discussed, with great hilarity, Sidney confessed that he had been unable to calculate the minutes that had been taken up by this rather preposterous second proposal. But he added that the moments when he ranted and while Charlotte failed to listen, seemed, at the time, to be endless. Of course they found their way around and over these obstacles and, imagine our heroine's relief upon hearing that Sidney was not (nor had he ever been) engaged to Miss Lambe.

"But the report I had was that Miss Lambe would very likely marry a gentleman who went to Eastbourne from Sanditon, a man with family in Sanditon," said Charlotte, perplexed.

Sidney laughed. "The man, if I am not mistaken, is surely our very own Sir Edward Denham."

"I did not know he was in Eastbourne! Did he not go to London? I thought it was you who was betrothed to Miss Lambe."

Sidney, now persuaded that Charlotte's feelings were all for him, was compelled to take her hand in his. "If you had only known how I suffered, you could never have made the mistake you did in believing *I* could ever love another."

"Likewise!" cried Charlotte defiantly. "Had you considered my anguish you could not have presumed *me* to be engaged to your brother!"

Such bewilderment as Charlotte and Sidney had endured was all the result of a few letters having gone between Miss Lambe and Mrs. Griffiths. Added to this was a pinch of misinterpretation on the part of poor Maisie. The unreliability of a writer with an injury to her wrist was not to be overlooked. Mrs. Griffiths's inadequate postscript had left the matter of Abigail and Arthur's engagement so poorly described as to leave it entirely open to conjecture. It was all highly alarming. A harp was to be considered a dangerous object indeed! Charlotte distinctly remembered Maisie telling her that Mrs. Griffiths's wrist limited the nature of her correspondence. No written report, unless it contained the utmost in detail and confirmed fact, was ever to be relied upon again. Women, then, were *not* the only correspondents to depend upon!

Charlotte and Sidney, quickly over their horror that such mistakes had been made, were soon inclined to reflect with gratitude on these trifling misunderstandings. For what, other than the misguided belief that Charlotte was to marry Arthur, would have brought her favorite back? If both Sidney and Charlotte were stubborn, then they were equally forgiving and within time, they concluded that Mrs. Griffiths and Miss Lambe had much to be thanked for, by being the main cause, inadvertently, of harnessing the pair of them together, finally.

It is considered foolish of a woman to expect a renewal of regard to occur in the heart of a man who has once been refused! It is thought that there is not one amongst the male sex who would not protest against the kind of weakness a second proposal to the same woman might imply. Some (even those whose opinions we admire) believe there is no indignity so abhorrent to the feelings of men. If that were the case, second proposals would be unheard of;

as it is, they occur frequently enough amongst the impassioned. Repeated proposals, scarce though they are, do happen and are generally a success so long as enough time has passed for the refuser to develop strong feelings of regret. When Sidney Parker, for the second time, proposed to Charlotte Heywood, he did so with grace, with genteel sincerity, and without any sign of amusement whatsoever other than a genuine soft smile. Charlotte was won at once. She accepted him, of course, and the two affirmed their devotion with the wordless affection that both had dreamed of savoring for so long.

There, dear reader, would be a natural and pleasing end to this tale of Sanditon and, if life could be fashioned in so neat and polished a manner as novels, I would have it (as the person responsible for relaying this tale) that "Finis" be written on this very page. We have the knowledge of a double wedding to rejoice in; most convenient for Mr. and Mrs. Heywood, for Charlotte and Abigail could not prevail upon their parents to travel to Sanditon on more than one occasion. No, the sisters must combine their weddings. There was no other solution. There was no other means by which to lure their mother and father from Willingden. But what a happy situation—there is scarcely a more favored conclusion to a tale that I can think of than that which sees two sisters marrying on the same day!

Additionally, we must gain some satisfaction in knowing that Mr. Parker and his cherished town are set for prosperity, but what of less passionate matters? Miss Lambe and Sir Edward Denham, it has been intimated, have formed a union. What of that circumstance? Could we bear to tear ourselves from this little part of the Sussex coast without first knowing more? And Maisie, we are acquainted enough with her now to be feeling a degree of fondness, are we not? I, in your position, would at least be eager to know if she became a great reader. Oh, and what of Lady Denham and her eager throng of potential beneficiaries? It would be a person in possession of a very dreary mind indeed who would not be inquisitive about that situation and I must confess I do not like the idea of writing for such dull elves.

And so, for the moment at least, we must spare Sidney and Charlotte our scrutiny. Anything else might, very rightly, be considered impolite. We need not worry, however, they have kissing and cooing enough to occupy them while we concentrate on the others who now intrigue us. Maisie, for all her devotion to reading and writing, could not possibly have become accomplished enough by the end of the summer to write a letter of several pages in length to Charlotte, but, write such a letter she did.

Chapter 29

Charlotte had given no thought to Mrs. Parker's tale of butlers and chambermaids. She was full in love with Sidney, greatly inclined to talk of dresses and wedding breakfasts with Abigail, and generally so taken up with the present that the past no longer held much fascination for her. It was all forgotten.

All that was forgotten by Charlotte, however, had been dwelt upon with regularity by the Raynor family of Heddingham House in Essex. Lady Raynor, whose sensibilities were perhaps more tuned than her husband's, had, even after a good deal of time had passed, lamented the loss of her good butler. And she had regretted the departure of her sweet-natured chambermaid with such deeply felt anxiety and grief as to render her quite stricken. Her husband's sympathies could be relied upon. He was not a man inclined to mournful reflection himself but his wife's heartache could not be ignored. On the matter of the removal of a good piece of family silver, he chose to remain silent. His wife, however, could not. Her refusal to allow that any member of their staff would steal from them was quite fixed. There was to be no argument.

Sir Thomas Raynor, ever sensible of his wife's affections for her departed staff, said only that he thought it a very great shame that such a scandal had visited them. He had grown disinclined to entirely trust anyone since the attempted seduction of his only daughter Rosamunde by a man from the South. His wife's protests in support of her dear Stafford (the butler) and her little Jane (the chambermaid) were heard with all the gentility he could muster, but with very strong feelings of hesitation. He was never to be easily persuaded of anyone's worthiness again. The possibility of deception on the part of one's staff, he decided, must by necessity be considered an uncommon but genuine risk. An employer's elevation could, he conceded, be viewed with avarice by dissatisfied servants. It was a constant peril and one he was never to be easy with. But, he would *not* lock away his possessions; he would *not* hide his silver.

He would, however, make it a rule to hide his daughter. Where she was concerned, every measure of protection must be employed. Poor Rosamunde Raynor. She was well past coming out age but had ventured nowhere. She was denied parties, only allowed to attend teas or suppers where the guests were known to, and approved by, her father and kept in such a state of seclusion that all of her former prettiness had faded. Her fortune, therefore, was her downfall. It was her keeper. It was the very thing that made her, as far as her father could see, the likeliest victim of abduction that ever lived. So, she was kept quiet, wretched, and out of harm's way in the great house on the Heddingham estate. If a young man called to see her father, Rosamunde was sent to her room for a rest, or to the library to pursue her studies, or to any other place in the house on any pretext whatsoever. So long as Rosamunde was out of sight, Sir Thomas's wealth, which represented the girl's eventual fortune, was out of mind.

That he made his daughter unhappy was unknown to Sir Thomas. She, ever mindful of the very great disappointment her susceptibility caused him, elected to carry on with sweetness, affection, and quiet obedience. Guilt and her father's oppression governed her. She never opposed his will, she never complained, not even to her mother who she knew to be openhearted, but she longed to breathe in life. She dreamed of dancing, of being allowed to feel the shoulder-to-shoulder bustle of a good party, and flirt a little with some nice young men. But it was not to be.

Lady Raynor, her daughter's compliance never questioned, feared more for the downfall of her chambermaid and her butler. There was something right in her fondness for her servants. Her daughter, she accepted, would one day marry, her servants, she was entirely confident, would stay with her always. They were worth cherishing. She cared for them, made them her family, and treated them with a real respect that some viewed as unnecessary and others viewed as admirable. Lady Raynor was not unfeeling, but, as poor Rosamunde never protested against the restrictions her father imposed upon her, she failed to recognize her daughter's torment.

The greater share of her, Lady Raynor's, compassion was reserved for her two dearly missed employees. To trace them, without any intention of reprimanding them, was her object. In truth, Lady Raynor found it impossible to believe that any kind of union between the two had taken place. Oh, it was the accepted explanation. It was the myth, the gloriously indecent legend that circulated the world, but Lady Raynor was intent on an alternative.

Well-connected persons like Lady Raynor are in the happy position of being able to afford hobbies. Where neither time nor money impose restrictions, pastimes are highly recommended. They keep the mind from deterioration and should be compulsory for women who have no inclination but to sit fondling pugs and fancying themselves frail. Lady Raynor disliked small dogs, never once considered herself frail, and therefore hurled herself into solving the mystery of her lost servants' whereabouts. She consulted local people, employed the children of her tenants to ask questions, and finally, when two small but significant clues had been provided by a local grain farmer and the driver of a post chaise respectively, she traced the absentees as far as London.

Her good butler was beyond what service would require of him. He had lost, along with his reputation, the control of his mind. But he was not to be deserted. He was being cared for by a certain Dr. Brown in a sanatorium in the town and Lady Raynor, satisfied that his care was, for the time being at least, adequate, wished to set about looking for her Jane. Dr. Brown was Lady Raynor's salvation. His wife, who greeted Lady Raynor with politeness and concern, showed every sign of sympathizing with her visitor's cause and every sign of fear for her husband should he not retire soon.

"He is a martyr to his work, Lady Raynor," said she. "But he cannot be forced. He only ever threatens to slow his career, but never to stop completely. I fear for him. I persuaded him to take a little break by the sea recently. We are only just returned; in fact, our being home is so recent that we have not yet unpacked all our trunks! That has been my only success. He will never take holidays. We have spent the chief of our time here. But, I am more hopeful now. My husband so enjoyed our journey into Sussex and dearly loved the little spot that we settled in and thinks it quite a good thing that I have the idea to go again."

All this was said with no indication on Mrs. Brown's part that she felt resentment, but her worries were to be respected. Dr. Brown had long passed youth but he had an enthusiasm, a passion for his work, which made him unable to give it up entirely.

In Dr. Brown's care were three men who might fit the description Lady Raynor gave. None answered to the name of Stafford however. One, on Lady Raynor's inspecting him, proved to be too bulky, too swarthy-skinned, and altogether too rough to be her butler. The next was too short, too roundedly fat and comical to be her butler but the last, she confirmed, was indeed her man. He had lost a little weight and it was greatly distressing for her to find that the man who had been with her family for all of her lifetime no longer recognized her.

"Your Mr. Stafford arrived with a young woman," explained Dr. Brown. "You know we have so many *attached* runaways here that at first it was thought that an unusual, dare I say, inappropriate alliance had been formed. That, you will be gratified to hear, was not the case. We make alarming assumptions in this business, Madam. We see many an unmarried woman with child here. Your Jane—you did say the name was Jane did you not?—well, she was different. She served more as a carer; her sweet nature made her a very good nurse. She was very attentive to Mr. Stafford. I must tell you, Lady Raynor, that he would only repeat the name Heddingham on arrival here. That is how the mistake in his identity came about. We have him down as a Mr. Heddingham! My assistant assumed it was his name and his companion did not correct us. But, and here is the only deception I am aware that she ever employed, *she* did not introduce herself as Jane. It seems there was much concealed."

Lady Raynor could not have been more pleased. She was beginning to think herself something of a sleuth. With Mr. Stafford so easily found she was confident that Jane would also soon be recovered.

London was not Lady Raynor's favorite place. Her house in Holland Park was elegant but she did not wish to stay there. It was easier, she concluded, to stay in an hotel, to order a good dinner without the complications that the organizing of one's town staff very often causes. She duly acquired herself good lodgings and congratulated herself on her good fortune, her determination, and her success. Mr. Stafford, she was satisfied, would be well looked after by Dr. Brown until such time as she could arrange for something more tender in the way of care for him. His well-being, she felt very strongly, was entirely her responsibility.

The hotel dining room was very fine indeed, and full. The liveliness provided ample diversion for Lady Raynor who, unaccustomed to dining alone, enjoyed the distraction that polite eavesdropping always brings. She took in all the particulars of her fellow diners. There were six families, several single young men, one old woman, and two men; one had the look of an eccentric about him and talked animatedly about matters of business. The latter two were soon intruded upon by two young women and their brother. There was great delight in the two groups being united. The meeting was obviously unexpected and sincerely thought to be fortuitous.

Lady Raynor heard, with the customary intrigue of the inquisitive, how one Lady Denham had fallen ill and how these three people (she thought she heard their surname as Hollis) would visit her. The report of the poor lady's ill health was given by the eccentric man who she heard addressed as Mr. Parker. Goodness, he was an enthusiast. He spoke at length about his hometown of Sanditon, could clearly not consider denying the ladies and the gentleman a single detail, and when his speech finally came to a close, it was agreed by all, and noted by Lady Raynor with interest, that Sanditon must indeed be the most wonderfully improved place in the world. It was undoubtedly a sanctuary. It was the very place that a poor butler ought to live out his days. Lady Raynor decided that inquiries must be made.

Alas, by the time Lady Raynor had finished what proved to be a very well presented fruit pudding, the Hollises and Mr. Parker and his companion had all left the dining room. Sanditon, though, was entirely lodged in her thoughts, it was very definitely the place she wanted for her poor old Stafford. She would investigate the possibility of settling him there. It was perfect. She had overheard Mr. Parker say that he meant to set a doctor up there. Dr. Brown had told her where Jane had gone and it was in her mind to visit her just as soon as she could ensure that inquiries about Sanditon could be made. But she could not be in two places at once and as her object was now Willingden Abbots she formulated a plan that would relieve her of the necessity of going to Sanditon straight away and afford poor Dr. Brown and his wife another well-deserved and much needed visit to the coast.

Wasting no time, the following day Lady Raynor paid her visit to Dr. Brown and Mrs. Brown.

The mention of Sanditon brought a look of surprise to the doctor's face. "But we know Sanditon very well, Lady Raynor," cried he.

His wife could do nothing but interject excitedly. "Yes, yes," she agreed. "You will recall my telling you about our little coastal respite? Well, *Sanditon* was the place! How is that for a funny thing."

Lady Raynor was all eagerness. "Then you can vouch for its suitability. I have it in my mind, having overheard talk of the spot, that it would be the very place for Mr. Stafford."

"There could be worse places. No, indeed," said Dr. Brown, "I think Sanditon ideal. Mr. Parker, who lives there, has plans for a resident doctor. Now here's a coincidence, he thought *I* might be persuaded."

"Oh yes," cried Lady Raynor, "I know of Mr. Parker's plans for a doctor. This is all working out perfectly." Something more occurred to her. "I was going to ask you to go to Sanditon to approve the place for me, but that is now unnecessary. You have already been and I think I trust your praise of it above anyone else's."

Dr. Brown's joy could not be concealed. "But I *shall* go to Sanditon again, depend upon it, Lady Raynor," said he with satisfaction.

His wife, her joy and relief evident, said, "Last night, Lady Raynor, my husband agreed to fix a date for his retirement."

Dr. Brown smiled. "We also agreed to fix on a place," said he, "for London is not easy on the senses of a redundant man and I have always longed to retire to the coast. It must be Sanditon."

CHAPTER 30

Charlotte had her letter and, before ascertaining who the sender was, noted that it was a very nice long letter and one that would have been worth all of two shillings and sixpence had it not been delivered by hand. It ran:

My dearest friend,

I can imagine your surprise at receiving a letter from me, I am sure you would never have expected one, although you are aware that I have, under Mrs. Griffiths's kind instruction, been engaged in lessons. My tutor says I learn fast and, although I am accepting undeserved praise, I have enjoyed her compliments. And I have welcomed the chance to confess my literacy. The truth is that I have long concealed my ability to write and read. That is my first confession and this letter thereby proves my deceit. Pray, Charlotte, allow me to prevail upon your good sense and tell you the reasons for my sudden revelation. My past, it is assumed, cannot be retrieved, my memories and all attempts at recollection useless. Oh, I have prayed for that to be the truth. Alas, I have all details of my own history stored, remembered, and regretted. Here I recount them to you.

I was in service some years ago. It was a fine household and good people provided for me, gave me chances at learning, and encouraged improvement not only in myself, but in other servants in their employ. Sir Thomas Raynor was a fine master and Lady Raynor showed me every kindness. The humblest soul was never too low for Her Ladyship's attention; the smallest matters were always attended to. Miss Heywood, you cannot imagine how aggrieved I am to be forced to remember the beneficence of that household, for I fear its recollection of me would be vastly different. That I have abused the Raynors' trust causes me the deepest regret. Can I ensure that you will read the remainder of this letter when you learn I am no better than a common thief? I pray you will endeavor to, for matters of greater import shall be revealed.

My dishonest act must be described. The butler, when I was in the employ of the Raynor family, was a Mr. Stafford. His attention to every detail, his conscientious methods, and his expertise cannot be praised enough. It has long since been rumored that his abrupt departure from Heddingham House was the result of a liaison, but I know, as no other can, that this is not the case. How can I be so certain? Because I am the supposed seductress. I beg you, Miss Heywood, know this to be false; there never was any such affair, never any such intention on my own or Mr. Stafford's part.

He had been suffering with bouts of illness when reason seemed lost to him. When these fits came upon him, he was unequal to even the simplest tasks. I was so fond of Mr. Stafford, we all were, he was the father of our below-stairs family, I wished to protect him, to conceal if I could the nature of his deterioration long before he confessed it to me. At last, I was taken into his confidence; straight lines of thought eluded him too often to be dismissed. His determination to leave Heddingham House was strong. I could not dissuade him, I pleaded with him to apply to Sir Thomas, to appeal to our master's fair sense and secure his future within the household. But to remain there in any lesser position than had been his for so long was more than Mr. Stafford's pride would stand. He could not abide the thought of remaining at the house in any lowly station. He had been butler for more than thirty years. The Raynors, I am convinced, would have been charitable, but for Mr. Stafford to have stayed, to have suffered the indignity of sympathy, would have damaged him. The condition that so impaired him worsened with considerable force, he wished no farewell, fearful that the potency of goodbye might soften him, lay him open to persuasion.

Mr. Stafford always had a night off on Wednesdays. He favored solitude and would walk the parkland in fine weather, it was his thinking time, he said. Mr. Stafford could think for hours. The particular Wednesday, details of which I shall recount for you now, is significant because it was the day my new life began. With so much else of my existence being invention you will not be too surprised to learn that Maisie is not my given name, I am rightfully Jane Tailor.

That Wednesday Mr. Stafford went about business in his usual manner, he left the house at five, as was his habit, taking his walking cane with him. His behavior was not unusual in any way and no one was alerted to its being the very last they would see of him. I was not so shaken by his absence for I was accustomed to his being gone on Wednesdays. I knew I should never see him again, he had confided as much to me, I comforted myself with the notion that the full reality of the matter would only impress me by morning.

I was wrong, it played on my mind; my sleep was light and disturbed intermittently. At around three of the following morning I was awakened by the sound of footsteps outside. Quiet footsteps. I was so afraid, Miss Heywood, there was no Mr. Stafford to call, beckoning him in times of crisis was the usual mode. If Heddingham House was to have an intruder then I must be the one to remove him. I was quickly dressed, by candlelight, but did not take the lamp downstairs with me. I went directly to the kitchens where I saw a movement in the meat closet. The interloper had been and was gone, missed by moments only, an empty hook swung in evidence of his unlawful presence. The kitchen was dimly lit at that hour; I had little time to think. I took up an implement as a means of defense and ventured outside. I saw a glimpse of the vagabond running from the grounds but he was swiftly out of sight. I heard someone stirring inside the house. If I had disturbed anyone, I could not own it, I had been quiet, the intruder had been quieter.

But the silence was soon broken by the cry of "fire" from a maid's room. I saw the beginnings of the blaze in the window and knew it to be my room, my candle, and my fault. There were only minutes before Mr. Stafford's absence was noticed as well as my own. The assumption, I knew, would be quickly made. I could not return there, I had not the authority to divulge details that would explain Mr. Stafford's departure. I ran the way of the vagabond and began a vagabond's life from thereon in. I had nothing to sustain me, only the clothing that covered me, and the soup ladle I had taken from the kitchen. My weapon was now my wealth, my only small chance of survival. I hid until dark in a field of maize and took my pseudonym from the crop. I was Maisie and the rest of her story, by way of Dr. Wellscott's narrative, you are familiar with. I could not return to the house. I could not betray Mr. Stafford's trust in me.

Charlotte could not read on. "This poor angel describes herself as a thief! To have been led by loyalty into such horrendous circumstances. But why am I confided in so suddenly?" said she quietly. "What induces this girl to reveal all she has tried so hard to conceal?"

Charlotte could hardly keep to each line in order but Maisie's hand assured:

" … an explanation for this outpouring, a reason, such as I am sure you seek, for my sudden desire to confess my sins to you. I have assured you that the Raynors were in every way compassionate employers. They are well-connected people of considerable fortune and Heddingham House was the venue for many elegant occasions. The family is widely known and liked. Of course, when I was in their employ I did not know of dear Sanditon, but by a coincidence, I had knowledge of one of its residents. Sir Edward Denham was above ten times a visitor to Heddingham House. His object was the Raynor's only daughter, Rosamunde. My recollection of him and of the Denham name I did not connect with Lady Denham. It was not until Clara Brereton revealed herself to be secretly engaged to him that recognition was mine. A secret engagement and the name of Denham immediately alarmed me. I knew, if it were the same Sir Edward Denham I had previously encountered, that trouble must abound. It was not until I realized, from your account of it, that Sir Edward Denham was in Eastbourne, where Miss Lambe is staying, that I felt strongly alerted to the idea that some scandal was afoot. I knew him to be secretly engaged to Miss Brereton, I had become, on my visits to Sanditon House,

something of confidante to her. She revealed her predicament to me, involved me in her distress, and told me of her desire for a public announcement and of his for utter secrecy. She had been afraid, many times, that Lady Denham would discover their alliance.

One occasion had truly alarmed her, the two, given to meeting in the grounds in a spot they thought quite concealed, were almost discovered together by Lady Denham herself. Sir Edward made a hurried escape but Clara could not, she met with an accident, stumbled, fell, and was only discovered by a resident some good while afterward. Even now, Clara is convinced that her aunt knows more of the situation. Imagine, my friend, how misled the girl is. If all this were not enough to prompt my writing then the following accounts will prove to you at once that I am no alarmist.

Sir Edward left his mark upon the Raynor family; his attentions to their daughter were never forgotten. Fortunately for her he was revealed as a scoundrel, banished thereafter and the girl recovered. I now have it from Mrs. Griffiths that Miss Lambe is engaged to him, this information is also deemed to be confidential but Miss Lambe and Mrs. Griffiths conceal nothing from one another. Do not think ill of Mrs. Griffiths by assuming she disclosed this last to me. She did not. She read to me from a letter in which details of it were conveyed, but was loyal enough to her charge to refrain from including me in this private matter. But, Miss Heywood, you will have guessed my offense. I can read and did so, when Mrs. Griffiths left the room to fetch a new book, I took up the letter and saw all that she had not read out. When it is thought you cannot read, you find yourself trusted in many situations that you ought not to be.

If I thought I merited such a privilege I would beg your advice about how I could ever make recompense for all my misdemeanors. Alas, I fear it is too late for me. So many deceptions impede me. I am to flee again, although my heart aches at the thought of leaving the one person who has been dearer to me than anyone else ever has. You will easily guess my favorite's identity as being my own employer. You see, a wicked heart like mine is still capable of loving, but I am no fool, I could never expect a man of his superiority to show any regard for me. I must be gone by the time you read this and wish only that you will forget me if you cannot find it in your heart to forgive.

Forgive me,
Your humble friend
Jane Tailor

CHAPTER 31

Plans where any deception is involved are as susceptible to change as plans where none exists. Maisie's intention to flee, unannounced, was only thwarted—so detailed was her strategy—by the sudden and startling deterioration of Lady Denham's health. Had not that fine lady taken up ill in the early hours then Maisie would have been free to leave Sanditon before daybreak without hindrance. Charlotte would have had her letter and, as was clearly stated in it, the girl would be gone. But she was not. Lady Denham, quite out of spirits and suffering a high fever, had summoned the doctor and his nurse to her bedside just two hours before the undisclosed departure was to have taken place.

Never was a patient's ill health so resented as that morning. Wellscott, it must be assured, was the very mark of professionalism, but Maisie, he noticed, was somehow altered, quite unusually reticent about succumbing to Lady Denham's request that she stay with her. Alas, stay she would. The relatives—the Hollises, Clara Brereton, and Esther Denham went about Sanditon House with somber attitudes. Each adopted an air of melancholy, of sad concern, which did little to disguise the feelings of expectancy that resided in their hearts. For it was certain Lady Denham was not to last till noon, and it was certain she could forecast as much herself. Notice was sent express to Eastbourne to urge Sir Edward's return, then the lady called each of her relatives present to her bedside for a private address. Miss Brereton was the first to be seen, Esther Denham followed, then the Hollis ladies. Finally, William was addressed.

To each of them in turn she declared, "I have done what is right and I wish you happiness." It was made clear enough that none should reveal to anyone else what little she had disclosed and each of them, now pondering her mysterious words, endured the long hours until her passing with potent feelings of ambition and exhausting thoughts of wealth. Lady Denham's last two hours were spent with Maisie, who, now startled by the reality of her patient's sad destiny, was inclined to give up thoughts of escape and compelled, by the sentiment of the moment, to appease her invalid and to be, in every sense possible, the best nurse the world ever saw. The feverish brow was deftly mopped, the flushed face affectionately cooled, the fragile hand held gently, the whole of the lady's weary body eased, and her dying wishes were granted.

"Someone must read to me, Maisie," the weak voice urged, "from the good Lord's book, allow me this one last luxury." Was the nurse to summon a reader? Or was she, without a single care or thought, to take up the Bible herself and read? She was indeed to do so. She began, quietly at first, her voice, unused to reading aloud for so many years, trembled with the first line but within a short time her eyes and her mind and her voice, in unison, tripped over the passages and she read with clarity, with joy, and with a true feeling of openness growing in her very being. When Dr. Wellscott returned to his patient, he saw his nurse, his good assistant, reading from John. The doctor, with curiosity and amazement, opened the door quietly but did not enter, nay he could not enter, so fixed to the spot was he by the sight of his Maisie reading. He was at once speechless, motionless, and hopeful. She noticed him, of course; the sick room is deadly quiet, the creak of a door is enhanced by its uncommon stillness, but she did not stop. Acknowledging him with a look that spoke of apology, guilt, and love all at once, she continued to read.

"In the beginning was the word," she declared and Lady Denham, her body failing but her mind still astoundingly sharp, found the will to open her eyes and speak before she laid her head to final rest. Looking with quiet determination at Dr. Wellscott, she mused, "A mutual love of reading, my dear man, is as good a foundation for a happy union as any I know." These were the last words she spoke; but before her eyes closed, her small audience of two detected something of jocularity in her tone of voice.

Pretty gardens and elegant drawing rooms are generally the favored venues for proposals of marriage. Sick room declarations of ardor are, to the best of all knowledge, unheard of, but it is a thankful truth that love has its way of obscuring ugliness from the eyes of its captives. Not that there was anything so wholly unpleasant about Lady Denham's bedchamber; as was to be expected, it was an elegantly appointed apartment, beautifully furnished and quite peaceful. Dr. Wellscott was compelled to propose in Lady Denham's presence, her knowledge of his feelings had been greater than his own, and he felt, singular though the idea was, making his offer in her proximity to be entirely appropriate.

It was something of a hurried invitation, for the matter of informing the relatives of Lady Denham's demise was not to be delayed. Suffice it to say that Maisie accepted with heartfelt exhilaration, the doctor gave her a single kiss on her pink cheek, and little more was to be said between the two of them until all the formalities of attending the grieving members of Lady Denham's family had been seen to.

There was a brief exchange on the stairs, when Dr. Wellscott, unable to contain his delight, said to Maisie, "You curious little creature, a bookworm all along, eh? That explains the mystery of my books seeming to move about in the breakfront by themselves."

Tragedy could not be felt! It might have been expected that a person as seemingly sprightly as Lady Denham would have lived longer; many others have determined to do so before her. Alas, she did not, but her death was judged, by at least three people, as having occurred at a most fortuitous time. Dr. Wellscott, Maisie, and Charlotte all knew, once the points of the matter had been discussed amongst them, that if Sanditon still had its great lady, it would not have its Dr. and Mrs. Wellscott. And *their* value was not to be underestimated.

CHAPTER 32

In life Lady Denham had been nobody's fool and her character in death was not about to alter, her Will and Testament delighted and disappointed, as was to be expected and the simplest way to give explanation of how the lady dispensed her fortune is to peruse the document that outlined the matter. It ran as follows:

Last Will and Testament of Lady Elizabeth Grace Denham

In the name of God, Amen.

I, Elizabeth Grace Denham, of Sanditon, East Sussex, in perfect mind and memory do make and ordain this my last will and testament, inform as follows, to witnesses:

To my niece, Clara Brereton, it is my will that she shall have the collection of lace collars in my possession at the time of my death. It has been my belief that a legacy such as this will prove useful and of some small sentimental value to her.

To Miss Esther Denham, I bequeath the sum of two hundred pounds. My suggestion is that she might consider pursuing a career in nursing; such has been her attentive kindness to me, during my last illness.

It is my dearest wish that Sir Edward Denham should be in possession of a greatly valued collection of verse, in various volumes, from the library at Sanditon House. His love of poetry exceeds any I have occasioned to witness in any other human.

To Eliza, Julia, and William Hollis, respectively, I wish to state that, due to their connection to my late husband Mr. Hollis, I have always felt very particularly toward them. In recent years, the importance of this connection has intensified in me and with that in mind I determined to have exact replicas of my late husband's portrait made in order that they would each have these mementoes to enjoy. These, I am sure, they will treasure.

Additionally, my entire estate, to include the sum of thirty five thousand pounds, land, and property, I bequeath to the town of Sanditon. It is my wish to appoint Mr. Thomas Parker as trustee of this legacy, which he must use to the benefit of the place by means of its promotion, improvement, and protection in order that others, for many years to come, might enjoy the advantages.

Lastly, I constitute, make, and ordain Dr. C. E. Wellscott the sole executor of this, my last Will and Testament, and I do hereby utterly disallow and revoke all former testaments, legacies, and executors ratifying and confirming this and no other to be my last Will, in witness whereof I have hereunto set my hand and seal, one thousand eight hundred and seventeen.

Signed, sealed, published, and delivered by the said Lady Elizabeth Grace Denham, as her last Will and Testament.

Can there be anything so shocking—so heartbreaking—to a fortune hunter as to see the coveted wealth given over to a good cause, a cause so decidedly removed from thoughts of luxury as would sicken a greedy heart? Esther Denham, who had always felt herself to be unsuited to the coast, opted for the sophistication of a house in town, preferring, what Mr. Parker rather harshly described as, "the filth of the Capital to the clean fresh purity of a seaside town." Clara Brereton was to remain, so too Sir Edward Denham, despite the exposure of his character and the revelations surrounding him and his multitude of secret engagements. In truth, he ended up being publicly disgraced and reviled by anyone who, due to his deceptions, had fancied themselves betrothed to him. He did not marry Miss Lambe. She, much to Mrs. Griffiths's delight, was later carried off by a widower of good fortune some fifteen years her senior whom she had met in Eastbourne. Miss Lambe (Mrs. Noble as she became) took on her husband's children, riches, and house with a seemingly natural flair. Visits to Sanditon were rare although she did much to recommend the place as being one of the jewels of the Sussex coast in her way of talking about it to her new acquaintances.

Sir Edward Denham remained shameless. He had engaged in flirtations, seductions of multiples of women, telling each one who he was secretly engaged to that these outward displays of alternative interest would serve to conceal their alliance. His character, his reliance upon his personality and charm, afforded him a degree of acceptance. Word of his scurrilous conduct soon spread and in its way contributed to a healthy fluctuation in Sanditon's business. Scandals are so well liked by society in general, any hint of drama or sensation is relished, it is comforting, for the flawless at least, to learn that others err, although quite why they are in need of such solace is something of an oddity. Mrs. Noble (née Lambe) eventually viewed Sir Edward Denham as little more than a comical figure, which, coupled with her new husband's attentions to her, allowed her to recover far more quickly than Mrs. Griffiths had ever expected.

"For she always appeared such a frail thing, poor tender child, to think of her being victim to a seducer quite rattles me."

With Mrs. Griffiths rattled, Miss Lambe settled, and the majority of the Sanditon residents in a general state of contentment it must not be overlooked that the Hollises, less grieved at their relation's death than they were by their inconsequential legacies, left Sanditon promptly with no goodbyes. Nothing was made of their having ever been there at all, they took their portraits of poor Mr. Hollis, and were not ever heard of again.

One Miss Beaufort felt herself crossed, the other felt them both deceived, for William Hollis, in a rather ungentlemanlike manner, failed to honor either of them with a parting gesture. The unfortunate Miss Beauforts, who had made such a promising start with their bright smiles, coquettish giggles, and pretty clothes, had suffered somewhat in their being *not* so in the middle of things as their characters craved. To endure an entire summer only for it to end in dull frustration had left them less sparkling and more in need of flattery and flirtation than ever before.

Sir Edward, now reduced in circumstance, presented no noticeable signs of retrenchment. His less than respectable pecuniary condition meant that debts mounted rapidly and credit was offered less readily than it otherwise might have been. Still he maintained an air of extravagance, boasting of plans for a house in town and of intentions to go to Italy where, he claimed, "the poetic is never overlooked." He kept himself to two rooms in Denham Place and took lodgers to bolster his income; thinking nothing of gambling what little extra he had at card tables. He could no longer bestow his attention on a young lady of any sense without inducing an element of caution in her heart. His intentions were thwarted by his character being known and the reduction of his circumstances.

The Miss Beauforts were different creatures altogether now; to secure interest of any sort from any type of man was their aspiration and the sisters, once again the object of Sir Edward Denham's overt attentions, would soon regain a little of their glow. Was there ever to be a proposal of marriage it is certain that foolish hearts would be broken. There was little to choose between the sisters and little now to recommend a fallen Sir, as opposed to an elevated Mr., so the three were destined, for the remainder of that summer at least, to linger, dissatisfied and discouraged, in a flirtatious impasse and make their own kind of wildly inappropriate happiness.

CHAPTER 33

Arthur and Abigail, Charlotte and Sidney, Maisie and Dr. Wellscott all married in Sanditon and all remained there. There was something about the place, without a doubt.

Must every neighborhood have a great lady? Sanditon had thrived to a degree with one, but did so now far better without one. Lady Denham's meanness had served Sanditon very well. Her legacy, albeit given in a spirit of posthumous retribution toward her family, did everything to lift the place. She became greater acknowledged in death than she had ever been in life. So much bad feeling could now be released. Lady Denham's poor relations were free to openly despise her for her final neglect of them.

Mr. Parker decided against a monument but, unable to overlook the need for a memorial of some kind for Sanditon's deceased patroness, deemed an annual garden party at Sanditon House to be the very thing. It was just the event to reel in visitors and such an appropriate way in which to celebrate the truly great difference the lady, not to mention her money, had made to the neighborhood. Mary Parker, who had always been a good deal more thoughtful than her husband, thought a garden party the most offensive form of tribute. "Poor Lady Denham's decline *began* at a garden party," she reminded her husband when the idea first sprang into his mind. "Would it not be imprudent, insensitive even, to commemorate her in such a way?"

Mrs. Parker, as usual, was ignored and carried with her very strong feelings of displeasure at the thought of the damage an annual garden party would do both to the lawns at Sanditon House and their, the Parkers', reputations. People were sure, she convinced herself, to think the idea wholly inappropriate. She felt very impressed by the notion that Lady Denham's spirit would be in a state of perpetual fainting unease at such an indignity.

Sanditon House itself, however, was to become something between an hotel and a place for convalescence. It was later to be renamed Waterloo Lodge which satisfied Mr. Parker's longing to use the name. Overseen by Dr. Wellscott and his wife and generally managed by Diana Parker, it proved a most successful business. It is said that the Prince Regent stayed there in pursuit of a means to recover from the effects of overindulgence. Certainly the wine list for the period, written records of an entirely odd centerpiece *(half water, half vegetation)* and a handwritten note by the housekeeper *(HRH requests 12 entrees for a midweek dinner)* suggest that there is truth in the rumor.

Furthermore, Mrs. Wellscott, in her 1819 diary, observed that the Prince Regent was "*just as Lamb has described him*" and that the "*monstrosity at Brighton*" would "*never be a public treasure, merely an embarrassing reminder of the excesses of its creator.*" "Prinny," as the droves of intimates who reportedly came to Sanditon to share his hospitality referred to him, was a wealthy, if unprincipled, guest. Thereby, Mr. Parker had succeeded in attracting the *ton*. Such visitors were not to be scoffed at; ladies, should they think themselves unequal to the sight of unclothed men seabathing, were advised to stay in their bathing machines, cover their eyes, or stay indoors. The wealthy, for all their eccentricities, were not to be discouraged on account of the sensibilities of the poor!

Mr. Woodcock, the keeper of the other hotel in the neighborhood, bore Waterloo Lodge no grudge. All the time it did not claim his business he was not inclined to resent its success. Moreover, he believed Waterloo Lodge promoted his own establishment. His regulars, those who could not afford the luxury of the Lodge, still came; so too did new faces. And these fresh visitors, either disappointed by Waterloo Lodge's "*No Vacancies, By Private*

Appointment Only" sign or unequal, financially, to securing rooms there would apply to Mr. Woodcock with every confidence of his receiving them with his customary politeness and warm welcome.

Waterloo Lodge's favored and permanent guest, however, was one Mr. Stafford, formerly of Heddingham House, who, on the advice of the now retired Dr. Brown, came to Sanditon to live out his days. He was dutifully and lovingly attended by Dr. Wellscott's good lady Jane, who saw to her patient's every need with full-hearted compassion and genuine feelings of fondness. Old Mr. Stafford often thought, when the mists of his mind temporarily cleared, that he had seen young Mrs. Wellscott's face before and this fleeting recognition was a comfort to him. He could not recall the night when the young chambermaid, quite dejected after a night in a cornfield, had discovered him by the roadside one Thursday morning. He had no memory of her accompanying him to London, no knowledge of her selling a fine piece of silver to a scoundrel for far less than it was really worth, and absolutely no idea that it was *she* who had placed him in the safe hands of Dr. Brown. It was never much talked about but it was generally known, in private Sanditon circles, that Mrs. Jane Wellscott had once been Maisie Granger, who had once been Jane Tailor.

Dr. Brown, whose retirement proved tolerable by his being made useful at Waterloo Lodge, only once spoke of Maisie's story. He confessed that his part in her deception had been to send her, with his full recommendation, to Willingden Abbots. A colleague of Dr. Brown's, a good doctor who was leaving the sanatorium to set up his own practice, agreed that Maisie would indeed make a fine assistant. Both were satisfied that she would make a good nurse. Dr. Brown's confession was given, with Mrs. Jane Wellscott's consent, to Charlotte Parker who, having had the greater part of the story in a letter could not settle until she had the rest. She had always been inquisitive, analytical, and there was nothing like an unsolved mystery to intrigue her.

CHAPTER 34

Lady Raynor's search in Willingden Abbots for her chambermaid had come to nothing. The doctors' practice had closed by the time she got there and the doctors and their nurse had departed. There was nothing to be done. One Dr. Kendall had gone away and no one in the neighborhood knew where Dr. Wellscott and his assistant had disappeared to. It was thought he had been destined for the North of England, but it could not be confirmed that he ever got there.

Her delight therefore on discovering, in a letter from Dr. Brown, that her dear little Jane was living in Sanditon, was immense. The letter, however, was scant in its detail. It was too much of general matters. Such brevity in correspondence was not to be accepted. How disappointing it is to pay the post only to find the chief of a letter taken up with the mundane. If one wanted particulars, one must find them out. To go to Sanditon became Lady Raynor's new scheme. She was determined to take her daughter, Rosamunde, with her. Once she had persuaded her husband and rid him of his propensity for strictness with every firm assurance of caution, this plan was approved.

Edward Denham's presence in Sanditon was not welcomed by the Raynors. On learning of his being there, Rosamunde made it clear she did not want to see him. He, likewise, had no desire to see her and he hid himself in the library, in his house, or in the drawing rooms of any young ladies who would have him whenever she was near. The avoidance was a success. Rosamunde Raynor and Sir Edward Denham only once laid eyes on each other and this was the cause of more pain to him that it was to her. Rosamunde

Raynor cared not for Sir Edward now that she had the attentions of one Lieutenant Smith who, despite his love of life on the ocean, found himself quite steady and satisfied with love on dry land. The thought of setting sail in the spring now held less promise for him.

When blue shoes were no longer the fashion, Mr. Heeley proved his acumen by producing slippers of different colors and boots of every style in every material. Mrs. Whitby's library prospered and her visitor list increased with each year that passed. She ensured enough of the Romantics filled her shelves and Edward Denham (the "Sir" so little suits him now that we shall dispense with it) was often seen there seeking out an excerpt, looking for a particular line and generally aiming to improve his eligibility by means of increasing his romantic appeal.

Arthur Parker improved so dramatically in health that Diana and Susan quite despaired of him. "All the years we thought him afflicted! To think, sister," said Diana, "that our whole lives were dedicated to his improvement to no avail. I do not resent the sacrifice, we did what we thought was right in the way of duty, but you know I now think we must blame Arthur, and Arthur *alone*, for our spinster states. We have wasted ourselves and our best years are gone, Susan. But he is so boisterous now, so unlike himself, I find it hard to believe he was ever so unspirited. It does seem, does it not, that his ailments were all in his mind."

Thank Heaven for Waterloo Lodge and its visitors. By this new venture the Parker sisters, completely resigned to ending old maids as Arthur had taken up the whole of their youth, kept occupied. There was a new Arthur to be seen to every week. And in the winter months, when the frail or antisocial sought to escape the dirt of London or the madness of the season, they found themselves permanently engaged, ordering hot milk possets and other restoratives. Each sister delighted in complaining, with the vigor of persons far more healthy than they would admit to being, that they felt themselves very poorly used indeed.

Arthur, now free of both his ailments and his zealous sisters' attentions, lost his inclination to be sickly along with the greater part of his appetite. Abigail Parker was no fusser. Arthur would have green tea if she served it and Arthur would live. Arthur's right side would not be stricken, numbed, or immobilized. Arthur, in truth, had never in his life stopped to think that he might be anything other than sick, but with a wife, and the fresh Sanditon air to uphold him he was never to look at a leech again. And, as for buttered toast, his penchant there remained unshakeable. Arthur Parker also discovered the joy of seabathing but was instructed by his wife, with the harshest of penalties threatened, that he must remain clothed in the water whatever the fashion dictated. In this, he was, thankfully, inclined to obedience.

One hot summer afternoon, many years later, when her children were at play in the garden and her husband was in his surgery attending to matters of business, Mrs. Wellscott happened to see from the drawing room window that a passing carriage, taking the road rather too eagerly, had overturned. A gentleman and his wife tumbled out. Both were unsteady and bruised. The gentleman, though, in attempting to walk, realized his injury—a sprained foot. When he had finished reprimanding the driver and satisfying himself that his wife was not harmed, he sat himself down, unable to stay standing.

"Something is not right here," said he, gesturing to his ankle. "But all will be well, my dear. This is the very place, if one must endure an injury. We couldn't have overturned in more fortuitous a spot. Soon we shall be assisted. There, I am sure, is the means to my recovery."

It is certain that the gentleman was right, for where better to be, if an injury is to be suffered, than Sanditon with its curative briny sea, cloudless skies, fresh air, and accomplished doctor? If ills can be ameliorated anywhere in the world, then Sanditon is the very place and this truth was never more clearly fixed in the mind of anyone than it was in Mrs. Charlotte Parker's. She, in her part of the town, was taking in the sight of the sparkling sea that had greeted her arrival as a single girl all those years before. She breathed the air and the essence of the place, heard the gentle waves rolling on the shore and the gulls screeching overhead, and knew no evils could survive in the good wholesome atmosphere of the place. White curtains fluttered at open windows, gay hats were worn by lady walkers, and smiles and greetings were exchanged along the promenade like gladly given gifts. Her husband often laughed about the place, it was a habit he was loathe to forego, but in his heart he acknowledged that it had something at once mysterious and bewitching and so entirely its own as to make him bound to stay there for the rest of his days.

The ailing were inclined to seek out the place and plunge themselves into the sea by way of a cure and the healthy were just as devoted to visiting it, but the main portion of the visitors came in search of something less definable, more elusive, and infinitely more satisfying if it could be found. They came in pursuit of love, of romance, of the steady yet passionate mutual devotion that Sanditon's husbands and wives enjoyed. Thus the place prospered and its people thrived.

Moreover, there was never any hint of scandal heard about the place again. But you will not be deceived so easily; that no hint of scandal was ever heard is not proof enough to say with surety that no sensation ever erupted there. If any praise is due, it is to the good citizens of the place that they guarded their business so well as to keep it confidential. If you ever go that way, to that spot, to that little part of the Sussex coast that lies between Hastings and Eastbourne, you would be best advised to remember that the sea holds many secrets; not least of them being a selection of letters. One lot, tightly bound with a satin ribbon and closely written in an amorous style by one "adoring Edward" to one "dearest sweet Clara," and another, less substantial batch, by the same author, in his usual provocative style to a Miss Lambe.

One more letter went to the waves, in tone and expression it was quite apart from the rest, penned in the summer of 1817 by a young woman who, it had been presumed, could neither read nor write.

There is one final thing, which is not to be overlooked: Lady Raynor, quite infatuated with Sanditon, always made it her holiday place. When others went to Bath, she went to Sanditon. She bought trinkets in the library, spending so much money that Mrs. Whitby, her confidence in her little business boosted by having such a generous and extravagant customer, improved her range and started a very lucrative line in silverware.

That a lost butler and a lost chambermaid could reunite so successfully with their former mistress was nothing short of astounding. That a soup ladle could likewise find its way back into the hands of its rightful owner is a little more astonishing.

It was, of course, recognized at once by Lady Raynor on account of its monogrammed H, and she made no quibble about paying Mrs. Whitby her price for it, saying only, "It is what is right, Mrs. Whitby."

Sir Thomas Raynor, on hearing of the recovery of his heirloom, was full of praise for his wife. "You amaze me, my dear," said he, "nothing is *ever* lost to you." His satisfaction at having his canteen complete again was short-lived, however, for his wife's intention to give the piece, as a gesture of her affection, to Dr. and Mrs. Wellscott was revealed. But he could not long maintain any bitterness of spirit. His daughter's youthful bloom had returned, she was to be married to Lieutenant Smith, and all levels of peace and harmonious living at Heddingham House were to be restored.

The sea at Sanditon is certainly bluer than any you would find if you traveled the length of the world, for the ink of a good deal of letters is run into it. But if the water tastes saltier on the tongue than the waters of other resorts, you might recall that many tears, shed more for pleasure than for pain, have been cried into it. Ah, Sanditon: all who enter there prosper or recover and some who enter there never depart.

Finis

ABOUT THE AUTHOR

Juliette Shapiro is an accomplished writer of both fiction and non-fiction whose work has been published by *Verbatim*, *QWF*, and *Jane Austen Regency Magazine*. She also writes pseudonymously as Yolande Sorores and was one of the contributors, using that name, to Flame Books' *Book of Voices*, a publication produced in support of PEN, the Sierra Leone charity.

She has enjoyed an enduring and dependable love affair with Jane Austen's works from an early age, and re-reads *Pride and Prejudice* at various junctures in her life, always finding therein something new to marvel at, laugh at, or take solace in. The unfinished *Sanditon* has long intrigued her.

Juliette Shapiro is the mother of two sons and two daughters. She takes laughable pride in being (to date) a grandmother to three glorious little girls and one beautiful boy, seeing as this achievement required no work or skill on her part. She thinks they are the most exquisite creatures on earth, but she is, of course, prejudiced. She was born in 1964 and named after a song.